THE BOBBSEY TWINS

THE MYSTERY AT CHERRY CORNERS

The Bobbsey twins are excited about visiting their cousins, the Parkers, who have just moved into a new home—a one-hundred-year-old mansion in Cherry Corners, New York. But no sooner do they arrive, when they are plunged into a mystery. The children of the area have been holding Pet Club meetings in an old schoolhouse situated at the far end of the Parker estate. But no longer, for all of a sudden, the old schoolhouse seems to be haunted. But is it really? Or is someone behind the ghostly antics, trying to keep the children away from their clubhouse? The Bobbsey twins are determined to find out!

Eagerly, they follow the trail of a kidnapped monkey which takes them on a thrilling chase through upstate New York. There they check out a hunch of Bert's and learn a startling fact about the man with the walrus mustache. With Danny Rugg on hand from Lakeport to add his own brand of mischief, the young detectives have their hands full. Danger and excitement make this vacation one they won't soon forget!

THE BOBBSEY TWINS

"I saw something dark moving onto the roof!"
Bert said

The
Bobbsey Twins:
The Mystery at
Cherry Corners

By

LAURA LEE HOPE

GROSSET & DUNLAP
A NATIONAL GENERAL COMPANY
Publishers   *New York*

CONTENTS

THE BOBBSEY TWINS

THE MYSTERY AT CHERRY CORNERS

CHAPTER I

THE HAUNTED
SCHOOLHOUSE

"HI, Patti! We want to see your monkey!" cried six-year-old Flossie Bobbsey.

She and her twin Freddie hopped out of the family station wagon as their cousin ran across the lawn to meet them.

"I thought you'd never get here!" exclaimed Patti Parker. She was a pretty eleven-year-old with curly brown hair. "We have a mystery for you to solve."

By this time the other set of Bobbsey twins, dark-haired Nan and Bert, were out of the car.

"We love mysteries!" said Nan. She and Bert were a year older than Patti.

"And monkeys, too!" said Bert, grinning.

"Where's Chuck?" asked Freddie.

"Here I am!" yelled a sturdy-looking boy of eight as he raced up with a big, shaggy brown dog. "Are we glad to see you! We want you to help us catch a spook!"

1

"A spook! Ooo!" said Flossie.

At that moment Mr. Bobbsey stepped from the station wagon. He was a tall, broad-shouldered man with a friendly face. "Hello, you Parkers," he said with a smile. "You, too, Cooky," he added, patting the frisky dog.

"Your new house is great, Patti," said Bert, looking up at the big white mansion with a tower on the roof.

"It's very old," she said. "More than a hundred years old."

Just then the front door opened and a young couple came out.

"Welcome to Cherry Corners!" called the woman, hurrying across the lawn. She was small and looked like Patti.

As she hugged the twins, her husband shook hands warmly with everyone. He was a slender man in dark-rimmed glasses.

Jim and Jessie Parker were Mrs. Bobbsey's cousins. The two families always enjoyed visiting each other.

This year the twins had been invited to spend four weeks of their summer vacation with the Parkers. Mr. Bobbsey, who had to go North on a business trip, had arranged to drop off his children on the way.

"We're sorry your mother couldn't come too," said Mr. Parker, patting Flossie's head.

"Mommy had to stay home 'cause our house is being painted," the little girl explained.

"Where's the monkey?" asked Freddie, tugging Patti's hand.

"Upstairs in our playroom," she said. "Come on."

Patti opened the screen door and led the way into the front hall. Chuck and Cooky followed.

A bright flowered rug lay on the floor. Next to the wide staircase was a telephone table.

"We just moved in three weeks ago," Patti said, heading up the polished steps. She explained that the house used to belong to her Aunt Emily Parker, who had died several months before. "Aunt Emily left it to us.

"We're not using all of it now," Patti went on as the children reached the first landing. "But Daddy's going to remodel the third floor into one big playroom. It'll be neat!"

"There are fifteen rooms," said her brother, "not counting the one in the tower."

"What's up there?" asked Freddie.

"Old boxes and stuff," replied Chuck.

"Aunt Emily never had any visitors," added Patti, starting up the next flight of steps, "so we haven't had a chance to explore before."

On the top floor, Patti led them down the hall and opened a door at the end. Cooky trotted ahead into a large sunny room with shelves of toys and books along one wall.

"Oh, there's the monkey!" cried Flossie. The young twins ran over to a large cage in front of the window.

"Hello, Milly," said Flossie

"Gosh! This cage is big enough to walk into!" exclaimed Freddie.

"Daddy built it," said Patti as she opened the door. "Come out, Milly, and meet the Bobbseys!"

The small black monkey swung herself onto Patti's shoulder, patted her little paws together and chattered. Cooky wagged his tail.

"She's just darling!" Nan exclaimed.

"Hello, Milly," said Flossie and put out her finger. The monkey grasped it. Freddie reached out his hand and she took it, too.

"Where did you get her?" Bert asked.

"Daddy bought her from a carnival that played here this spring," said Patti.

"Never mind about Milly," said Chuck impatiently. "Tell 'em about the spook."

"Chuck and I belong to the Cherry Corners Pet Club," said Patti. "We meet in an old abandoned schoolhouse, but the trouble is, it's haunted. We told the rest of the club that you were detectives and they want you to solve our mystery."

"We'd love to try," said Bert eagerly.

"Let's go, then," said Chuck. "There's a special meeting in a few minutes."

Patti went to a doll dresser and took out a small yellow sweater with matching shorts. She put the clothes on Milly and then brought out a red collar and leash. She fastened them around the monkey's neck.

"Oh, let me carry her," said Nan.

Patti handed over the pet, who climbed onto Nan's shoulder. Holding the leash tightly, she led the way downstairs.

Mr. Bobbsey was on the porch talking to Mr. and Mrs. Parker. After he had shaken Milly's paw, the children explained where they were going. He wished them luck, kissed the girls and Freddie good-by and patted Bert on the shoulder.

"Have fun!" he called as they hurried down the steps. Patti took them around the house, across the big yard and downhill through an orchard overgrown with weeds.

"These are our cherry trees," said Chuck.

Just then they heard barking and whistling from below. Cooky woofed and bounded ahead.

"Hurry!" cried Patti. "The others are already there."

The children began to run and soon came out to a wide, level clearing on the bank of a narrow canal. Near it stood a small gray frame building with a belfry. About a dozen children were waiting in front of it with animals on leashes, in small cages or in baskets.

"Look! A parrot!" exclaimed Freddie. He pointed to a large cage on a coaster wagon.

Suddenly Milly let out a screech and leaped from Nan's shoulder, jerking the leash from her hand. In a twinkling the monkey was on top of the cage poking her paw in at the big green bird.

"Stop it!" called a large redheaded boy who was running toward them. The parrot squawked loudly, spreading his wings in fright.

"Milly, no!" cried Patti.

As the cousins raced forward, the boy lifted the monkey off the cage. With a grin, he handed the pet to Patti.

"This is Bill Dugan," she said, "president of the Pet Club." She introduced the Bobbseys.

"Hi," said Bill, grinning. "This is my parrot, Pete. He gets along with everyone but Milly. When he sees her he screams."

Chuck laughed. "Milly teases him."

Meanwhile, the other children had gathered around to meet the Bobbseys. Patti took a large old iron key from the pocket of her jeans and unlocked the door of the little school. Bill went in first, carrying the parrot's cage.

The Bobbseys followed him up two steps into a cloakroom which ran across the front of the building. Beside the door hung an old rope.

"What's that for, Bill?" asked Freddie.

"You pull it to ring the school bell."

"Don't touch it," said Chuck quickly. "We'll tell you about it later."

Bill led them past a row of coat hooks and through an open doorway into the classroom. The other children crowded in, bringing the animals. They seated themselves at old-fashioned desks that faced the blackboard. Bill took his place at the teacher's desk on a platform.

"The meeting will come to order!" he announced. "I will call the roll. Answer for yourself and your pet. Sally," he began.

"Here," said a girl of ten with long blond braids. "Fritzi, too." She patted the dachshund on the seat beside her.

"George."

"Here," said a chubby boy of the same age. "So's Snoozy." In a cage on his desk was a bright-eyed hamster.

Next came George's younger brother Bob with a large white rabbit, then three smaller boys with a dozen turtles in large plastic containers. A plump ten-year-old named Mary held a cat she called Whiskers.

The last member to be called was a tall boy whose name was Slim. "I'm here," he said, "with my mouse."

As a small pink nose twitched over the top of his shirt pocket, Freddie giggled.

Flossie raised her hand and Bill nodded to her. "What do you do in the club?" she asked.

"We read up on our animals and give reports on how to take care of them," Bill replied.

"And we help each other," George spoke up. "Like when Whiskers got stuck in a tree and we all helped to get him down."

Suddenly, from above their heads came a loud clanging!

"The spook!" cried Sally. "He's ringing the bell!"

"Come on, let's catch him!" exclaimed Bert. He dashed for the door with the club members at his heels. As he rushed into the cloakroom he saw the bell rope going up and down, but no one was pulling it!

"It's ringing by itself!" cried Nan, unable to believe her eyes.

"This is not the first time," said Patti.

Bert stepped toward the rope. The next moment the schoolhouse began to shake.

Screaming, the younger children raced from the building. The older ones ran back to rescue the animals, then fled helter-skelter into the yard. As soon as everyone was out, the house stopped shaking.

While the others chattered excitedly, the Bobbseys, and Patti and Bill quickly circled the building looking for some sign of a mischief-maker. Then they searched the woods on either side of the clearing. They found no one.

"There never is anyone," said Bill. "That's what's so spooky."

After the Bobbseys had promised the club members that they would do their best to catch the "ghost," most of the children went home.

The turtle owners invited Freddie and Chuck to go catch frogs with them on the canal. As they hurried off, Bert asked when the haunting had begun.

"A week ago," Patti replied.

"The floor shaking is something new," said

Bill soberly. "The spook's really getting rough."

"Who owns the schoolhouse?" Nan asked.

"We do," said Patti. "It's on our land."

Flossie listened for a while, then wandered off. Reaching the canal, she saw that a wide level path had been cleared all along the bank, through the overgrown weeds.

Just ahead was a huge clump of bushes at the edge of the water. As the little girl paused, she heard a rustling sound.

"Maybe there's a big frog in the bushes," Flossie thought. "I'm going to try to catch him." She knelt down and put her head under the thick branches. Deep amongst the leaves, she saw two shiny eyes. They were much too large for a frog.

"Maybe it's a rabbit or something," Flossie thought.

"BOO!" she said. But the eyes did not move! They went on staring at Flossie!

CHAPTER II

MONKEY MISCHIEF

FRIGHTENED, Flossie pulled her head out of the bushes. She ran up the canal bank to Freddie and Chuck. Breathlessly she told them about the big eyes she had seen.

"It was probably just a rabbit," said Freddie.

The boys were lying on their stomachs looking into the water for frogs.

"There's one!" whispered Chuck. Cautiously he brought his hands down toward the big green creature with its golden eyes.

SPLASH! The frog leaped free.

"You missed him!" said Freddie, giggling. Then he made a grab at another frog.

"Ha-ha-ha! Missed him yourself!" said Chuck.

Flossie was disappointed that the boys would not listen to her. She walked back to the clearing. The older twins were seated under a large oak tree with Patti and Bill, talking about the ghost. Flossie quickly told her story.

"If it was just a rabbit, it should have run away when I said BOO. Maybe it was the spook."

"Let's find out," said Bert.

Flossie led the older children to the big clump of bushes. While Bill and Patti lifted some of the branches, Bert and Nan crawled underneath. After looking carefully, they backed out and stood up, brushing twigs from their hair.

"Nothing there, Flossie," said Nan kindly. "It must have been a rabbit."

Just then a whistle sounded in the distance.

"That's Daddy!" exclaimed Patti. "It's time to go home."

The two frog hunters came running up.

"We had no luck," said Freddie, wiping his wet hands on his blue shorts. "All the frogs got away."

"So did my spook," said Flossie.

They hurried back to the schoolhouse. While Patti locked the door, Bill loaded Pete's cage on the coaster wagon and started down the wide path along the canal.

"See you tomorrow," he called as he disappeared around the bend with the younger boys at his heels.

Going up through the orchard, Milly rode on Nan's shoulder while Cooky trotted ahead.

"I don't see any cherries," Freddie said, looking up into the leafy branches.

"These are old trees and they don't have fruit

any more," Patti explained. "But there's a big orchard at the south end of town. It has lots of them. We live in cherry country."

"What do you mean?" Flossie asked.

"Most of the cherries in New York State are grown around here."

Reaching the house, the children told Mr. and Mrs. Parker about the ringing bell and the shaking schoolhouse.

Mr. Parker shook his head. "Somebody's playing a joke on you."

His wife nodded. "The person is going to a lot of trouble, though," she remarked. "I wonder why."

After the children had washed their hands and faces and combed their hair, the family seated themselves in the big, cheerful dining room.

"Umm, everything looks yummy!" said Flossie as Mrs. Parker served fried chicken and creamy mashed potatoes.

For dessert she brought out a large cherry pie. "I'm practicing for the Cherry Festival," she said with a smile.

The Parkers explained that each summer the town of Cherry Corners held a two-week festival which, it was hoped, would draw lots of visitors.

"Everybody in town works to make it a success," said Patti. "The ladies bake pies, some of the men make souvenirs, and we have a parade.

Daddy writes lots about it in his newspaper," she added. The twins knew that Mr. Parker owned and published the *Cherry Corners News*.

Chuck spoke up. "And Mr. Brewster, who runs the riding stable, dresses his horses in fancy harness and gives carriage rides. It's lots of fun!"

Mrs. Parker sighed. "But I'm afraid it's not much use," she said. "Every year we get fewer visitors. There are too many other attractions in New York State."

"A lot of tourists go to the Baseball Hall of Fame in Cooperstown," said Chuck. "It's a small village with many different kinds of museums in it. One is all about baseball and has statues of famous players."

"People also go to Watkins Glen," Patti added. "That's a beautiful, deep gorge."

"Yes, and there are some old-fashioned villages around. They've been restored to look as they did hundreds of years ago," added Mr. Parker. "Cherry Corners can't compete with all that."

After supper the children went for a walk with Milly and Cooky. At the first corner they turned right onto Main Street.

"Let's go see the O'Neals," said Chuck. "Maybe they'll let us help them with the souvenirs."

Patti explained that sometimes in the evening she and Chuck visited their friends, Mr. Fred

O'Neal, the carpenter, and his son Mike. "They make lots of things out of wood."

"Especially boats," Chuck put in eagerly.

"You mean real boats that go in the water?" Freddie asked.

"All kinds," said Chuck, "from fishing boats to tiny toy ships in bottles. And they also carve little animals out of wood."

"Those are sold at the Festival," said Patti. "We varnish them. It's fun."

She stopped before a two-story gray frame building with a red door. Over the brass knocker was the sign: O'NEAL & SON. Patti knocked twice, then led the way inside.

At one end of the room a small fat man was seated at a long workbench with his back to them. As he spun around on a little stool the visitors saw a friendly face with pink cheeks and a fringe of gray hair encircling a bald head.

"Hello there, Parkers," he said cheerfully. "Are these your detective cousins?"

"Yes," said Patti. As she introduced them, a tall, black-haired young man came through a door at the rear.

"This is my son Mike," said Mr. O'Neal proudly.

"I never met twin detectives before," the young man said, his eyes twinkling. "Do you solve double mysteries?"

The Bobbseys laughed. "Tonight we just came to work on the animals," Bert replied.

"Well, we're always glad to have a little help, aren't we, Dad?" said Mike.

From a shelf behind the bench he took down several cans of varnish and some brushes. The children helped him carry them to the far end of the workbench where there was a tray of small carved pieces.

"Oh, aren't they bee-yoo-ti-ful!" said Flossie. "Look at the dog and the pussycat!"

"And a giraffe and even bunches of cherries!" Freddie chimed in.

As the children sat down on a long bench, Milly crowded in beside Patti. Cooky flopped down behind them. Carefully Bert and Nan opened the cans of varnish, and everyone began to cover the wooden figures. After a minute Milly reached for Patti's brush.

"No, no," said Patti to the monkey. She put the brush down and placed her pet on the floor. "You stay right there, Milly, and be a good girl."

After a while Freddie got up and walked down to watch Mr. O'Neal work. He and his son were making the small model of a boat.

"That's funny-looking," said Freddie. "Why is it so wide on the bottom and round on one end?"

"This is a model of an old Erie canalboat," Mr. O'Neal told him. "It's the kind that used to run on the feeder down by the schoolhouse."

The twins looked puzzled. "What's a feeder?" Freddie asked.

"It was a small canal that emptied into the big Erie Canal," Mr. O'Neal explained, "which ran from Albany to Buffalo. At the time it opened in 1825, the Erie Canal was the longest one in the world. It carried people and merchandise to the West and brought raw materials to the East."

"How fast did the boats go?" Freddie asked.

Mr. O'Neal laughed. "Very fast, son. The speed limit was four miles an hour!"

The children giggled. "That isn't very fast," said Freddie.

"It was for those days," Mr. O'Neal answered. "You must remember that these boats were pulled along the canal by two or three horses walking along the towpath."

Chuck spoke up. "You know the wide trail that goes along the canal by the schoolhouse? Well, that's the old towpath."

"Yes," said Mike, "and young fellows just about Bert's age used to drive the horses. It was a summer job. In the winter the canal was closed."

"Is the Erie Canal still there?" Flossie asked eagerly. "Could we take a ride on it?"

"Yes," Mr. O'Neal said as he carefully fitted a roof to his little boat cabin. "The channel has been made wider and deeper and parts of it have been moved. But the canal still goes from Al-

Freddie knocked a pot of glue onto the floor

bany to Buffalo. There are several other branches of it, too."

"Lots of freight barges and private boats use it," said Mike. "But, of course, none of them are pulled by horses any more." He smiled. "The whole thing is called 'The New York Barge Canal System.' "

Nan was about to ask a question when Cooky suddenly began barking. The children whirled to see him dashing across the room with the monkey on his back. In the monkey's hand was a brush dripping with varnish.

"Milly! Put that down!" Patti cried.

The children laughed so hard that Freddie knocked a pot of glue onto the floor. "Ugh!" he said.

Bert collared the dog, while Milly dropped the brush into his fur and leaped free.

"Oh, Cooky, your hair is all icky!" said Patti, trying to get the brush out.

"Wait now," said Mike, "let me help you." He picked up a pair of large shears from a shelf. As he cut the brush out of the shaggy hair, Cooky woofed.

Mike grinned. "Don't worry, old boy. I didn't take off much hair."

Patti sighed. "I don't know what I'm going to do with that monkey! She's always picking up things!"

Milly was now on the floor under the workbench. "Aren't you ashamed of yourself?" Patti asked sternly. The monkey hid her face in her hands. In spite of themselves the children laughed.

"It's no use!" said Nan. "She's too cute. You can't scold her."

Flossie scooped the animal onto her lap. "You're a bad little girl, Milly, but we love you."

After helping the O'Neals clean up the shop, the children said good night and left for home.

On the way they stopped at a soda shop where everyone had ice cream cones, including Milly. Chuck bought a small package of cookies for Cooky.

"He just loves these," said Patti. "That's how he got his name."

By the time they reached the Parker house the cones and cookies were gone. As the children came up the walk, the front door suddenly opened. Mrs. Parker looked out.

Seeing them, she smiled and called, "Hurry, children! I have a surprise for you!"

CHAPTER III

SPOOK HUNTING

"YOUR mother's on the phone," said Mrs. Parker as the Bobbseys ran up the porch steps.

The twins hurried into the front hall, Chuck and Cooky close behind them. Patti followed with Milly on her shoulder.

Nan picked up the telephone. "Hello, Mother!" she said happily. At the same time the others crowded around and called out hello.

"Is something the matter?" Nan asked.

"No," her mother said with a chuckle. "I just wanted to talk to you. I miss you all already."

Mrs. Bobbsey spoke to each of the children. Bert was last. At first he smiled, then as he listened, the boy frowned. At last he said good-by and hung up.

"Anything wrong?" Nan asked him.

"Danny Rugg is coming to Cherry Corners."

Freddie groaned. "That pest!"

"Who's Danny Rugg?" asked Mrs. Parker.

"I think I know," said Patti. "Didn't we meet him the last time we visited Lakeport, Nan?"

"He's that big, mean kid," Chuck spoke up. "I remember him."

The Bobbseys explained to Mrs. Parker that Danny liked to pick on other children and was especially unfriendly to the Bobbseys.

"Mrs. Rugg met Mother in the grocery," said Bert, "and told her that she and Danny were taking a trip to Cooperstown and Watkins Glen. They expect to stay awhile in Cherry Corners because Mrs. Rugg has a friend here."

"Well, don't worry about it," said Mrs. Parker. "Danny may not cause you any trouble."

"You don't know Danny," said Freddie and sighed.

As the boys went off to watch television, the girls took Milly upstairs to the playroom.

"Would you like to undress her?" Patti asked, handing the monkey to Nan. "I'll get her bed ready."

While Nan and Flossie carefully took off Milly's sweater suit, Patti stepped into the big cage and went to a doll bed in a corner. She fluffed up the pillow and folded back the quilt. Then Nan put the monkey into the bed.

"Now go to sleep like a good girl," said Patti as she and Flossie pulled the quilt up around Milly.

"She's just like a real baby," Flossie said.

As the three girls left the cage, the monkey

made chirping noises. Patti latched the door and turned out the light. Then she led the way to her room. Nan and Flossie would sleep with her.

"It's so bee-yoo-ti-ful!" said Flossie. She loved the pink curtains and white furniture.

Soon the older girls were settled in the twin beds. Flossie sat cross-legged in her pajamas on a cot and listened as they talked about the schoolhouse mystery.

"We must examine every inch of the place," said Nan firmly, "especially the belfry."

"Daddy has a big ladder," said Patti. "I'm sure he'll let us borrow it."

Next morning at breakfast Mr. Parker gave his permission. While the young twins and Chuck played with Milly on the back porch, the others took the ladder from the garage and carried it down through the orchard.

"Wait a minute," said Bert as they neared the bottom of the hill. "Let's look around first to be sure no one's here."

Quietly the children put the ladder down, slipped into the clearing, and circled the schoolhouse. They peered through one of the windows. There was nobody in sight.

"Let's go inside," Nan suggested.

While Patti unlocked the door, Bert and Nan brought the ladder. They carried it into the cloakroom and propped it against the wall. Straight above them was a trapdoor with a hole in one side for the bell rope to come through. In the middle of the hole was a metal ring. Bert climbed up and pulled hard on the ring. The rusty hinges creaked and the trapdoor swung down. With it came a shower of acorns and dry leaves.

"Ugh!" Nan cried as she and Patti jumped back.

Above them they could see the big black iron bell. It hung from a wooden beam in the open-sided turret.

"You girls go outside," Bert said. "I'll move the bell back and forth while you watch the belfry and the roof. See if you can spot any wires or strings. There must be some kind of rigging which makes the bell ring without the rope being pulled."

As Nan and Patti obeyed, he climbed to the top of the ladder, reached up and took hold of the bell. It was heavy, but he began to move it back and forth. As the clapper hit the sides and a clang sounded, he could see nothing unusual. When he gave it a harder push, the bell swung wider and pulled him off his feet.

"Help!" he yelled and kicked wildly. His foot hit the ladder and CRASH, it fell! Bert was hanging from the rim of the bell!

"Nan!" he shouted, hoping the old beam overhead would hold his added weight.

The next moment the girls burst through the open doorway. "Hang on!" cried Nan. "We'll get you down!"

"Hang on!" cried Nan. "We'll get you down!"

She and Patti set the ladder up against the wall. Then they guided Bert's dangling feet to a rung. He let go of the bell and climbed down.

"Thanks!" he said with a grin. "Did you see any rigging?" They shook their heads.

"We'd better search the rest of the school," Patti suggested.

Carefully the three children examined the floors, walls and desks. They found nothing which might explain the spooky ringing or the shaking of the house.

"Maybe there's something under the building," Bert said. "Let's check."

The children went outside and walked around the frame structure. They saw some small broken places in the old boards near the ground. Bert took a pencil flashlight from his pocket, shone it in a hole and peered into the darkness. The thin beam of light swept back and forth, showing rough earth and stones.

"Nothing there," Bert said, sitting back on his heels. "It's just a space under the floor. There's no opening big enough for anyone to get in to plant a trick device."

"Unless there's a loose board," Nan said.

The children searched but found none. Finally they went back inside and Bert climbed up to close the trapdoor. As he lifted it, there was the sound of breaking wood and the door came off in his hands. "Take it!" he exclaimed, almost dropping the heavy wooden piece.

The girls grabbed the door from him.

"I guess the spook didn't come in through the belfry," Patti said. "That hasn't been opened in years."

"Besides," said Bert, climbing down, "the openings in the turret aren't very big. I doubt if a man could squeeze through one."

After the two had carried the ladder outside, Patti locked the door.

"I just can't believe in spooks," Bert said as they started toward the hill. "There has to be another explanation."

"I think someone is trying to scare us out of our clubhouse," said Patti, "but I don't know why."

"Whoever's playing these tricks," remarked Bert, "is very good at it."

When they reached the back yard of the house, they were delighted to see a large blue plastic swimming pool at one side. Mrs. Parker was filling it with water from the hose. The young twins were standing by, watching.

"Mr. Parker put up the pool this morning," Freddie called.

"Oh, Mommy! When can we go in?" Patti asked happily.

"This afternoon," she replied. "It's almost full now. We'll wait for the sun to warm up the water a bit."

Just then Milly leaped off the porch. The next moment she was on Nan's shoulder.

"Come here, Milly!" cried Flossie, grabbing for the monkey.

With an excited screech the pet jumped away and fell SPLASH into the water! The startled animal screamed.

Quickly Freddie scrambled up the ladder on the side of the pool. "I'll save her!" he cried and jumped in. He grasped the struggling monkey, and handed her over the side to Patti.

"Oh, Milly, you bad girl," said Patti, holding the dripping monkey away from her.

"Don't blame Milly," said Mrs. Parker as Freddie climbed out. "You must watch her more carefully."

"I fastened her leash to the porch rail," Flossie spoke up.

"But she's very good at opening knots," said Patti. "I should have warned you."

While Chuck and Bert put the ladder back into the garage, Freddie dried himself. Meanwhile, the girls rubbed the shivering animal with Flossie's towel.

"We must be sure she's dry," said Patti. "Monkeys catch cold very easily."

After Freddie had changed into dry play clothes, the children had lunch in the kitchen with Mrs. Parker. The older ones told about their morning's adventure.

"I have an idea," said Bert. "I'll hide my camera in the schoolhouse, attach a thread to the shutter and stretch it across the doorway. If our spook comes in, he'll trip over the thread. A flashbulb will go off as the shutter clicks open. Then we'll have a picture of him!"

"That's a great idea!" exclaimed Chuck and the others agreed. "We'll all go."

After lunch Bert took the Polaroid camera from his suitcase. When he reached the back porch he found Milly perched on Patti's shoulder in her yellow suit, ready to go along. Cooky was napping in a corner.

"Now go quietly," Bert warned as the six started for the hill. When they reached the clearing there was no one else around.

Quietly Patti unlocked the door and the children filed into the clubhouse. Milly jumped on a desk.

As Bert inserted a bulb in his camera, there came a hoarse shout from outside. *"Help! Help!"*

"Listen! Somebody's in trouble!" Nan said.

Bert put down the camera. "We'd better go see!"

As they dashed out, no one saw Milly pick up the camera and hang the cord around her neck.

Patti, remembering her mother's warning about the monkey, stopped to lock the schoolhouse door. She could hear the other children in the orchard calling, "Hello! Where are you?"

As she ran up to them, Nan said, "We can't find anyone."

Suddenly they heard a loud screeching.

"That's Milly!" Patti exclaimed. "Oh, something's happened to her!"

The children raced back to the schoolhouse. Patti gasped. The door was standing open!

"But I locked it!" she cried.

The children dashed inside. The cloakroom was empty. So was the schoolroom. The monkey and the camera were gone!

CHAPTER IV

THE SEARCH

"SOMEONE'S stolen Milly!" Patti exclaimed.

"I'll bet it was that old spook!" Chuck said angrily. "He called for help to get us out of the schoolhouse and then sneaked in to take Milly."

"And Bert's camera!" Nan added.

"Maybe there are two spooks," Bert suggested. "One lured us away while the other one stole the monkey and the camera."

Patti said nothing. Her eyes were full of tears.

Nan put an arm around her cousin. "Don't cry," she said kindly. "We'll find Milly."

"Did you say you locked the door before you ran out?" Bert asked.

Patti nodded, biting her lip.

"Then the thief must have a duplicate key," Bert remarked. "Unless he came in through a window."

"He couldn't have," said Chuck, "because

they're stuck shut. We tried to open them lots of times but couldn't do it."

"Maybe Milly got away from the spook," Flossie said hopefully. "She might be outside somewhere."

For half an hour the six cousins searched through the orchard and up and down the towpath calling the missing monkey, but there was no sign of her. Finally they went back to the schoolhouse. Sadly Patti locked the door, put the key in her pocket and the children returned to the house. They told Mrs. Parker what had happened.

"This has gone too far for a joke," she said, frowning. "I think we ought to call the police." She telephoned headquarters at once.

Ten minutes later the family was waiting on the porch when a patrol car pulled up at the curb. A tall young policeman with blond hair got out and came up the walk. He introduced himself as Officer Wright.

The older children recounted to him how the monkey and the camera had disappeared.

"I'll check the place over," he said. "You wait for me."

"Here's the key," said Patti sadly, giving it to him.

After a while he came back. "It would not be hard for someone to have a duplicate key made for that door," he said. "All the person would have to do is take a wax impression of the lock and have a key made from that." He frowned. "But I can't see why anyone would go to all that trouble just to get into an old schoolhouse."

The children told him about the spooky tricks. Officer Wright looked thoughtful. "Someone must be playing a joke on you," he said. "But this is not funny." Then he smiled at Patti. "Try not to worry about your monkey. We'll put out an alert for her."

After he had left, the anxious cousins searched the neighborhood for Milly.

"It's no use, I'm afraid," said Nan. "Poor Milly must be a prisoner some place."

"And the worst of it is," Patti added, "that even if she gets free, she won't know her way home. We've lived in this house only a little while."

At supper, they told Mr. Parker what had happened. He looked grim and said, "If I catch this joker, I'll make him sorry he ever did it."

That evening Bert telephoned the news to Bill Dugan. The president of the Pet Club suggested that all the members search for Milly the next day.

"I'll call them," he added. "We can use the dogs for bloodhounds."

"It might work," said Bert. "We may pick up a clue anyway."

In the morning the children dressed in blue jeans and shirts. After breakfast they hurried down the hill. Chuck had fastened a clothesline to Cooky's collar. Nan was carrying the quilt from Milly's bed. The other children were arriving when they reached the schoolhouse.

"I brought Pete," said Bull Dugan as he came up pulling the wagon with the parrot cage on it. "He can keep watch here. He'll squawk if he sees Milly."

Bert sent most of the searchers off in pairs. Then Nan let both dogs smell the monkey's quilt. After they had sniffed a few moments, Fritzi trotted off into the orchard with Nan, Patti, Flossie and Sally following. Cooky headed for the towpath with Chuck holding the lead and Bert, Freddie and Bill following.

"One of the dogs must be wrong," remarked Freddie.

"Remember, they're not real bloodhounds," said Bert.

Five minutes later the boys rounded a bend in the path. To their left stood a ruined stone chimney amid brush and high weeds. Suddenly Cooky gave a low growl and strained toward a big bush.

"He's found her!" whispered Freddie excitedly.

The next moment the dog jerked loose and dived under the bush. There was a scurrying noise and suddenly a small brown rabbit dashed out with Cooky chasing it.

"Watch out!" yelled Bert, as the big dog ran into Freddie. The little boy sat down hard and

"Watch out!" yelled Bert

Cooky bounded away with his rope dragging.

"A rabbit!" said Bill in disgust.

Freddie got to his feet and looked around. He spotted several foundation stones amid the weeds.

"What is this place?" he asked.

"An old grocery," said Chuck. "There used to be stores and houses along this canal bank a hundred years ago. That's when the schoolhouse was used."

"You can find lots of interesting stuff around here," Bill put in. He picked up a piece of rusty iron. "Like this old barrel stave. Once I found a brass weight from a scale."

As he spoke, Bert's eye was caught by something shiny lying on a stone beside the ruined chimney. He walked over and picked it up.

"Look at this!" he said. It was a small screwdriver. "This is brand new!"

The other boys crowded around. "That's funny," said Bill. "Who would leave one of those in this out-of-the-way place?"

"Maybe the spook dropped it," said Freddie.

His brother shrugged. "Could be." He slipped the screwdriver into his pocket. "Anyhow, I'm keeping it for a clue."

As the boys started back toward the schoolhouse, the dog came loping down the towpath, his ears flopping.

"Cooky, you're useless," said Chuck sadly. The big dog barked and wagged his tail.

Bill grinned. "The only things he can find are cookies."

They walked back to the schoolhouse where the girls were waiting on the stoop.

"It's no use," said Nan with a sigh. "Fritzi just isn't a bloodhound."

"Neither is Cooky," said Bill.

He turned to the parrot, which was sitting quietly on a perch. "I guess you didn't have any luck either, did you, Pete?"

Soon the other searchers came drifting back. No one had found a sign of the monkey. After telling Patti that they were sorry, all went home, except Bill.

"I keep thinking that Milly could have escaped from the spook," said Nan, "and might find her way back here to the schoolhouse. We ought to set a watch."

"That's a good idea," Bert replied. "We'll hide in the orchard and leave Pete where he is. If he gives the alarm we can run out and catch Milly."

"But suppose the spook comes," said Freddie. "He might kidnap Pete."

Bill chuckled. "I don't think so. This bird would be hard to steal because he'd make too much noise."

It was agreed that the boys would stay on guard, while the girls went home.

"We'll ask Mrs. Parker if we can make some sandwiches for you," said Nan.

The three girls hurried back to the house, taking Cooky with them. Patti's mother approved their idea.

"Nan, you and I will prepare the lunch and you can take it down to the boys," she said. "Patti, I'd like you to go to the store for eggs and milk."

"I'll go, too," said Flossie.

Soon she and her cousin were hurrying along Main Street. In the middle of the block was a large gray frame building with a peaked roof and wide double doors. At the curb a thin man in overalls was filling a long stone basin with a hose.

"I remember that place," said Flossie. "There are horses inside."

"Right. It's the riding stable," Patti replied, "where people used to hire carriages in the old days. Now it's mostly a garage, but Mr. Brewster keeps some horses for people to ride."

By now the two girls had reached the stone trough. Mr. Brewster smiled at them as he turned off the hose. "There now," he said, "we have fresh water for our horses."

"May we see them?" Flossie asked.

"Sure. Come pay us a visit sometime." He rolled up the hose and walked back inside.

Just then a loud voice cried, "HONK, HONK, HONK!" The girls turned to see a big boy riding his bicycle toward them on the sidewalk.

"Danny Rugg!" exclaimed Flossie.

Grinning, the boy from Lakeport steered straight at Patti.

"Be careful! Stop!" Flossie screamed.

With a cry Patti jumped backward, but too late. Danny swerved, but the rear wheel knocked her over.

CHAPTER V

THE NOISY CHIMNEY

"HA-HA-HA!" Danny called back as he pedaled away on his bicycle.

"Danny Rugg! You're mean!" Flossie called after the boy. She turned to help her cousin stand up. "Did you get hurt?"

"No, but I'm all dirty. And I'd like to tell that Danny what he is. And he's not supposed to ride on the sidewalk anyway."

"He's just terrible," said Flossie.

She helped Patti brush herself off, but there were mud spots on her face, hair and clothes from where the watering trough had spilled over.

"I can't go into the store looking like this, Floss," she said. She dug some money out of her pocket and gave it to the little girl. "Here, you get the eggs and milk. I'll go home and change. Do you mind?"

"Course not," said Flossie, feeling important. "You go on home."

Twenty minutes later she arrived in the kitchen with the groceries. Patti and Nan were helping Mrs. Parker fix lunch for the girls.

"I took the boys' sandwiches down to them," said Nan. "They found a good hiding place. They're behind the bushes in back of the big oak."

Flossie eyed the platter of peanut butter and jelly sandwiches on the table. "Umm," she said. "Those look *so* good."

"Well, let's sit down and eat them," suggested Mrs. Parker, chuckling.

While the others ate hungrily, Patti only picked at her food. "Maybe we ought to go down to the schoolhouse after lunch," she said anxiously. "We could help the boys watch."

Flossie looked disappointed. "Aren't we going in the pool?" she asked.

"I think we might as well," said Nan. "The boys don't want us. They said not to come down, because if the spook was around he might hear us and be scared off."

"That's a good idea," said Mrs. Parker. "I'll go with you. It's certainly hot."

"While we're swimming," said Nan, "we can listen for the parrot. If he screeches we'll run down and help the boys catch Milly or the spook."

"Maybe both of them," said Flossie hopefully.

An hour later Mrs. Parker and the three girls were in their swimsuits splashing in the water.

After a while Patti and Nan climbed out and lay on the soft green grass to sun themselves. Mrs. Parker went into the house.

Soon afterward, Nan said, "Shh! Listen! I think I heard the parrot!"

Both girls were silent. "Flossie, be quiet a minute!" Nan called.

Flossie climbed out of the pool and perched on top of the ladder. "What's the matter?" she asked.

"I think I heard something. Listen!"

All three strained their ears and the next moment they detected faint screeching from down the hill.

"That's Pete!" cried Nan, jumping up. "He must have seen Milly!"

She and Patti slipped on their sandals and started running toward the orchard.

"Wait for me!" cried Flossie, scrambling down the ladder. She wiggled into one of her slippers. The other was gone. For a few minutes she hopped around looking for it. At last Flossie found the shoe under a bush. She fished it out and put it on.

By this time the older girls were gone. Flossie ran across the yard, and down into the orchard.

"Wait for me!" she called, but there was no answer.

Panting, she reached the bottom of the hill and burst out of the trees into the clearing. Only Bill was there, leaning over the parrot cage.

"What happened?" Flossie asked excitedly. "Did Pete see Milly?"

"We think so," said Bill. "We were hiding in the bushes and all of a sudden we heard a funny noise. It sounded like Milly crying except it was kind of muffled. Then Pete began squawking. He had heard her, too. When we ran out he was flapping all over the cage, but there was nobody around."

Bill looked worried. "If Milly had been free she'd have jumped on Pete's cage and we would have found her there. She never misses a chance to tease him. I think the spook was sneaking around here carrying her in a bag or something."

"Poor Milly!" said Flossie sadly. "I wonder why the bad man is carrying her around?"

Bill looked puzzled. "I don't know. I've been thinking about it. He must be taking her somewhere. But this is such an out-of-the-way place, why would he come down here?"

"Maybe he wants to give her back," said Flossie hopefully. Her eyes grew wide with excitement. "Did you look in the schoolhouse?"

"She's not there," Bill answered, shaking his head. "We looked through the window."

"I hope the spook doesn't turn her loose in the woods," said Flossie. "There might be bears to eat her up. Course little baby bears wouldn't hurt her," she added quickly. "Milly could play with them."

"Are there bears in these woods?" Flossie asked

"That's a dangerous thing to do," said Bill. "Don't you ever try it. The mama bear is usually close by and she gets very angry if you bother her cubs."

"Are there bears in these woods?" Flossie asked.

"No," said Bill, "I never heard of any."

"Where is everybody else?" Flossie looked around.

"They're trying to track down the spook."

"Which way did they go?"

Bill pointed down the towpath. "That way. I wish I could have gone with them," he added, "but I have to stay here in case the fellow comes back."

Flossie left him, ran down to the canal and trotted along the path, calling to the others. There was no answer.

When she came to the ruined foundation, the little girl stopped in surprise and stared at the stone chimney. "I never saw this before," she thought.

Suddenly Flossie heard a scraping noise. She jumped.

"That sounded as if it came from the chimney," she told herself. The next moment she heard a rattling and scratching.

"Maybe something's caught in there," Flossie thought.

She moved timidly toward the chimney. Suddenly there came a louder scraping. Frightened, Flossie ran back to the path.

"It's something big," she thought. "Maybe it's Milly."

Flossie was about to go back again when another idea struck her. "S'pose Bill was wrong and it's a little bear, and there's a big mean mama bear around somewhere?"

For a moment Flossie stood undecided, then she raced forward along the towpath. As the little girl rounded the bend, she saw Bert stooping at the water's edge, examining the ground.

"There's a noise in the chimney!" Flossie cried excitedly. "Come quick! Maybe it's Milly —if it's not a bear!"

Bert looked up. "Take it easy, Flossie. You're all out of breath. Now say it again."

Pink in the face, Flossie repeated what she had heard. "Where is everybody? We ought to tell them."

"Not so fast," said her brother. "The others have gone on ahead to see if they can find any clues. I was just checking for footprints."

"Did you find any?" Flossie asked anxiously.

Her brother shook his head as he stood up. "No. Maybe the others have had better luck. So come on, we'll take a look in the chimney."

"What was that place where the chimney is?" asked Flossie as she trotted beside Bert.

"It's an old grocery." Bert smiled at his little sister. "You're sure this isn't just more imagination, Flossie—like the eyes in the bush?"

"No," said Flossie seriously. "I really did see the eyes and I *did* hear noises in the chimney."

"I'm sure you did," said Bert. "But I think they were rabbits or squirrels."

In a few minutes they reached the ruined foundation. Bert put his fingers to his lips. For a moment the two stood quiet, listening. All was silent.

Bert moved through the high grass toward the chimney with Flossie close behind him. He knocked softly on the stones of the chimney. There was no response.

"Get a long stick," he said.

Flossie looked around in the grass until she found part of a branch. She brought it over to her brother. He was on his knees near an opening at the bottom of the chimney, looking up into it.

"Do you see anything?" Flossie whispered.

Bert sat back. "There's something stuck in there all right," he said. "When you look straight up you can't see the sky through the hole at the top."

He took the stick and poked it up into the chimney.

Flossie clasped her hands. "Be careful," she said.

Bert jabbed harder and there was a scraping sound. "I'm getting it loose," he muttered. "It's going to fall."

Flossie stopped beside her brother as he thrust the stick in harder. Suddenly he jerked back.

"Watch out!" he exclaimed. "Here it comes!"

CHAPTER VI

"YOW!"

AS Bert pulled Flossie back, a brown box dropped from the chimney. He pulled it out onto the grass beside them.

"It's a pet carrier!" Flossie exclaimed. "The kind people use to carry little dogs and cats in."

"But it's broken," said Bert. "See, the window screen in one end is pushed out." He shook the box and looked inside. "It's empty."

"Milly was in there!" said Flossie excitedly. "Look!" The little girl picked a bit of yellow fuzz off the broken screen. "From her sweater suit!"

Bert nodded. "Yes. Whoever kidnapped Milly must have put her in here and stuck her up in the chimney. What a mean person!"

"But Milly got away!" said Flossie, clapping her hands. "Good for her!"

Just then Nan's voice sounded a little distance away. Flossie ran to the towpath, telling her sister to come fast. Moments later Nan ran up to the ruin followed by Patti, Freddie and Chuck. They all examined the carrier as Bert explained what had probably happened.

"My guess is that the spook heard us coming after him and wanted to dump Milly fast, so he pushed the box up the chimney."

"Perhaps he'll come back for her," Chuck suggested.

"Somebody ought to stay here and keep watch," said Nan.

"I wonder why he brought her down here?" Patti asked.

"My guess is," said Chuck, "that he couldn't keep her any longer. Milly could make a lot of trouble," he added, grinning. "I'll bet the old spook found that out!" The children laughed.

"I'm so glad she got away!" Patti exclaimed. "But now she's loose and probably won't be able to find her way home again."

Nan looked thoughtful. "Even if Milly doesn't know the way to your new house," she said, "maybe she'll go to your old one."

"That's an idea!" said Bert. "You and Patti hurry over there and check. I'll hide here and watch the chimney."

"Somebody had better run back and tell Bill what happened," Patti said.

"I will," Freddie spoke up.

"And I'll go with you," said his twin.

"So will I," said Chuck. The three raced back

to the clearing and reported the whole story.

"I should help Bert," said the club president, "but I can't leave Pete here alone."

"Let us take him home for you," Freddie offered.

Bill smiled. "Would you do that?" he asked. "Gee, thanks. Chuck knows the way."

As he hurried off, Chuck started pulling the coaster wagon with the parrot toward the towpath. He walked down it in the direction away from the ruined chimney. The young twins followed, looking out over the narrow canal. The water was dark green and high weeds grew along the banks.

"What's on the other side?" Freddie asked. "Another path like this one?"

"Yes, but it's called a berm path," said Chuck. "It's narrower than this one." As they rounded a curve Freddie stopped short.

"Oh-oh!" he said quietly and pointed ahead. Some distance in front of them was Danny Rugg, throwing stones into the water.

"I hope he doesn't make trouble for us," Flossie said softly.

"Don't be afraid," said Chuck. "We'll just go ahead and not pay any attention to him."

As the three started forward again, Danny looked up and saw them. A grin spread over his face. He walked up and stood in front of them with his feet far apart and his hands on his hips. The children stopped.

"Yow!" cried the bully

"Where are you going with that creepy-looking bird?" Danny asked.

"He's not creepy," said Freddie, "and we're taking him home." The younger boys started to pull the wagon around the bully.

With that Danny stopped and picked up a stick from the path. Quickly he thrust it between the bars of the cage.

"Stop that!" cried Freddie as Pete gave a loud squawk and backed along his perch.

"You're scaring him, Danny," said Flossie.

The big boy grinned. "So what? I don't care!" He shook the stick again.

"Hey, cut that out!" said Chuck, pulling at Danny's arm. Pete flapped wildly around the cage.

"He'll hurt himself!" Flossie cried. "He could break a wing!"

Danny just laughed and poked harder.

"Listen, Danny, that's a very dangerous parrot," Freddie said, trying to scare the bully.

"Dangerous!" The big boy grinned. "This dumb bird?"

Freddie got an idea. "If you don't think he's dangerous just stick your finger in there," he said. "Go ahead, I dare you."

Danny threw the stick away and stuck his finger through the bars. Pete backed farther into the corner. Danny laughed.

"Oh, yes, he's dangerous, all right! Ha-ha-ha!" But as he said the last *ha* Pete darted forward and pinched the boy's finger in his beak.

"YOW!" cried Danny. He jerked his hand out and clutched his finger.

The younger children laughed. "Come on now, Danny, he didn't hurt you," said Freddie.

"No," said Chuck. "He can nip harder than that!"

"I think maybe we ought to let the parrot out," said Freddie boldly, "so Danny can see how dangerous he is."

"You wouldn't dare!" said Danny sullenly.

"Yes, we would, too," Flossie added.

As the big boy stood scowling, Freddie stepped closer to the cage. He put his hand on the latch. "All right, Pete, I'm going to open the door and you can come out now."

Suddenly Danny turned on his heel and raced down the towpath. As soon as he was around the bend the three children giggled.

"You really scared him off, Freddie!" said Chuck.

The little boy grinned. "But I don't know what I would have done if he hadn't run, 'cause I was afraid to let Pete out. He might have flown away."

Flossie chuckled. "Well, Danny certainly flew away!"

The three children continued down the towpath and soon came to Bill Dugan's yard which bordered on the towpath just as the Parkers' did. They pulled the wagon through Bill's long back yard up to the door and rang the bell. Mrs. Dugan, a small, pretty blond woman answered. She took the parrot cage inside and thanked the children for bringing Pete home.

When the three got back to the Parker house the girls and Bert were on the back porch. There was no sign of Milly.

"You didn't find her?" Freddie said, disappointed.

"No," replied Patti, "but we talked to our former neighbor, Mrs. Dell, and she promised to let us know if she sees Milly."

"No one came to the chimney, either," said Bert.

Flossie spoke up and told about meeting Danny Rugg and his nipped finger.

As the listeners laughed, Bert said, "That was a great idea, Freddie. You really got the better of Danny that time!"

After supper the children played with a big rubber ball on the front lawn until it began to grow dark. Then they sat on the porch steps talking about the mystery.

Bill Dugan rode up on his bicycle. He hopped off and dropped it on the lawn.

"Hi!" he called, striding up the walk. "What's new?"

"Nothing," said Bert. "What do you know?"

"I just had two phone calls," the club president replied. "George said that his mother won't let him come to the schoolhouse any more until the spooky business stops. Also Dick Wood called—the littlest kid—he has turtles, remember? His mother won't let him come either."

The other children looked worried. "I'm afraid if we don't solve the mystery soon," said Patti, "the club will have to find some other place to meet."

"That would be too bad," Chuck replied, " 'cause the school is a groovy clubhouse."

The others agreed.

"Somebody wants us out of there, all right," said Bill gloomily, "but I can't figure out why."

The downcast children talked for a little while longer, then suddenly lightning flickered in the sky. A moment later they heard a distant rumble of thunder.

"It's going to storm," said Bill, standing up. "I'd better be going." He mounted his bicycle. "See you tomorrow!" He pedaled off.

A few minutes later the first raindrop smacked on the walk, and the children hurried inside. After watching television for a while they went to the kitchen and had milk with freshly baked molasses cookies.

As they were drying the glasses, Freddie suddenly remembered that he had left the ball in the yard.

"I guess I'd better bring it in," he said uncertainly as the thunder rumbled.

"I'll go with you," Bert offered.

The brothers hurried through the house and

out the front door. The light rain had stopped, but the lightning was still flashing.

"Where did you leave the ball?" Bert asked.

"Over there by that tree," said Freddie. He trotted across the lawn beside his brother. Bert pulled a pencil flashlight from his pocket and aimed the beam along the ground.

"There it is," he said.

"Your flashlight's weak," Freddie remarked as he picked up the ball.

"I know. I need to get new batteries." Bert turned off the light and slipped it into his pocket.

The boys hurried back onto the front porch. There Bert stopped short and grabbed Freddie's sleeve.

"Listen!" From the shrubs beside the steps came a loud crackling of twigs.

"Something's in there!" Freddie whispered. "Maybe it's Milly."

Bert whistled softly, then called, "Milly?"

All was silent.

"I guess not," said Bert. "It must have been a squirrel or something." The boys went into the house.

The girls had already gone upstairs. They were seated on their beds in pajamas talking about the schoolhouse mystery.

Suddenly there came a loud crash of thunder and then a splash of rain against the window. Patti jumped up, ran over and closed it.

"Now it's really raining hard," she said.

The three girls looked out the window. As the lightning streaked across the sky, it cast a weird glow over the empty yard below. They could see the treetops tossing in the wind. Then thunder cracked. Flossie covered her ears and looked scared.

"Don't be afraid," said Nan kindly.

After a few minutes she tucked the little girl into her cot and kissed her good night. Then the older two hopped into their own beds.

Soon Patti and Flossie were sound asleep, but Nan kept thinking about the strange happenings in the schoolhouse. All at once she sat up with a start. *What was that noise?* Then it came again —*tap, tap, tap!* on the window!

CHAPTER VII

THE BANANA TRAP

NAN'S heart thumped with excitement. What could be tapping at the window?

She slipped out of bed, tiptoed over to it and cautiously peered through the pane. Nothing there but the darkness! Quietly she raised the sash and screen and leaned out. The rain had stopped, but the wind was blowing.

Next to the window was a heavy wooden trellis which ran from the ground to the roof. It was covered with a thick wisteria vine.

"Maybe somebody was climbing up or down the trellis," Nan thought, "and knocked against the upper windowpane. There's no screen on it."

She looked toward the roof but could see nothing. A little distance below her was a clump of wisteria larger than the rest. It was shaking.

"Maybe someone's beneath it," she thought, "though it could be only the wind moving the branches."

For a while Nan watched and listened. But she neither saw nor heard anyone. At last she went back to bed.

In the morning after breakfast, she told Bert and Patti what she had heard. "The noise was sharp—like a piece of metal hitting against the glass."

"Let's take a look around the foot of the trellis," said Bert. "Maybe we will see some footprints."

The three hurried out the back door and around the side of the house to the wisteria vine. There was a patch of mud around the bottom of it.

"Look at this!" Bert exclaimed. He pointed to a tiny human-like footprint.

"Milly!" Patti and Nan exclaimed together.

"She might have been climbing down when she tapped on your window, Nan," Bert said, "but she also could have been on her way up. If so, maybe she's still on the roof!"

"How can we get up there?" Nan asked Patti.

"Through the tower room! Come on!"

Patti ran around the house with the twins behind her. As they hurried into the front door they met the younger twins and Chuck.

"Where are you going?" Freddie asked as the trio dashed up the stairs.

"Maybe Milly's on the roof!" Nan cried. "We're going to see."

The younger children pounded after them.

On the top floor Patti led them to a door in the center of the hallway. She opened it, revealing a short flight of stairs.

"Quiet now!" said Bert sharply.

With the others behind him, he tiptoed up the stairs and carefully raised a trapdoor at the top. He glanced around a small square room which had windows on four sides.

"She's not in here," Bert said as he climbed up into the tower. "But look!" he exclaimed as the others followed.

He pointed to a partly opened window. The sill was wet and on the dusty floor were tiny wet footprints like the ones they had found in the mud below the trellis.

"But how did she ever get that window open?" Freddie asked.

"Easy," said Chuck. "She didn't. It's stuck. I guess it's been open a long time."

"Maybe Milly's still out on the roof," Patti said hopefully. "Let's see!"

She put her head out the open window and called, but there was no answering scurry of feet. The monkey was not in sight.

Disappointed, the children looked around the small room. Underneath one window was a large old-fashioned portrait of a man with a white beard. Here and there were a few worn boxes.

"Who's this man?" Flossie asked, stooping before the gold-framed painting.

"I don't know," said Patti.

"Maybe his name is on the back," Nan suggested.

The girls tilted the heavy, dusty picture away from the wall.

"There's something written on the paper backing," said Nan. The faded handwriting said: *Captain William Parker.*

"I know who that was!" Chuck exclaimed. "He was our ancestor, a canalboat captain."

"Yes, and when he retired, he built this house," Patti added.

"Daddy told us about him," Chuck went on. "He owned a packet called *The Erie Belle.*"

"What's a packet?" Freddie asked.

"It was a canalboat that carried passengers," Chuck answered. "There were many packets running on the canal in olden days. There are no more now."

"Look at this!" Nan said.

Between the picture and the wall she picked up a book with a worn red leather cover. Nan opened it and read the faded writing on the first page.

"It's the captain's log," she said.

The young twins looked surprised.

"That's not a log," said Freddie. "It's a book."

Nan smiled and said, "A log is a special kind of book. It's the record of a journey. Ship captains and airline pilots keep them."

As the other children crowded around to look, Nan carefully turned the pages. Here and there they were able to read the handwriting. The last entry was the clearest. Nan read it aloud:

"July 9, 1845—Today my beloved boat, *The Erie Belle*, burned at her moorings in Albany. I was able to save only two treasures: this log and the . . ."

Nan stopped. "The last word is blurred," she said. The others peered at it but could not make it out either.

"What could the second treasure be?" Flossie asked.

"Since the log is here, the other treasure might be, too," Chuck suggested.

The children looked in several boxes which were piled in a corner. One held old curtains, the other rolls of wallpaper. The third, a cardboard hatbox, had a pink cord handle attached to its sides and was tied with a string. They removed the lid and found it empty.

"There's nothing else up here," said Nan. "Let's show this book to your mother. Maybe she can guess what the other treasure is."

The children hurried downstairs with their discovery. Mrs. Parker was dusting in the dining room. She looked at the log with interest as the children told her where they had found it.

"Do you think the other treasure was gold or silver like pirates had?" Freddie asked eagerly.

Nan read, "July 9, 1845—the *Erie Belle* burned.
I saved two treasures—"

The others laughed and Patti's mother said, "Maybe it was just something that Captain Parker liked so much he called it a treasure."

"Whatever it was, the treasure would be very valuable now," said Nan, "because it's a relic of canal days."

Mrs. Parker nodded. "That's right." She smiled at the Bobbseys. "Are you detectives going to try to find it?" The twins smiled and nodded.

"Now we have two mysteries to work on!" said Flossie. "Won't Mr. Parker be s'prised when we tell him!"

"Yes, he will," said Mrs. Parker. "For the time being, we'll keep this log in his desk. If you find the other treasure, we can give both of them to a museum."

"I wish we knew more about canalboats," said Nan. "We need to know what kind of things were carried on them. Is there a library in town?"

"Yes, let's go there right now," said Patti.

She and Chuck led their cousins up to Main Street. At the end of the first block they turned into a side road. Near the corner was a white frame house set some distance back from the sidewalk. Over the door was a sign: *Cherry Corners Public Library*.

The children hurried up the walk. When they reached the front door their faces fell. A small hand-lettered card tacked to it read:

On Vacation—Back in Two Weeks. Marie Fenster.

"Oh, wouldn't you know!" said Patti. "That means we won't have any library until she returns."

"Is she the only librarian?" Freddie asked.

Chuck nodded. "The whole library's only one room in her house," he added. "Our town is pretty small, so we don't need a big one."

The children turned around and started home again. On the way Bert paused in front of a food store.

"I have an idea," he said, eyeing a display of bright shining apples, pears and other fruits. He picked out a bunch of bananas and came out with them in a brown paper bag.

"What are you going to do with all those?" Freddie asked curiously. "I could eat one right now."

"They're not for us," said Bert. "I'm going to set a trap for Milly. If she climbed up into the tower once, she might do it again."

After lunch he carried some of the bananas upstairs. The other children followed.

On the way he asked, "Patti, do you have a toy bell?"

She stopped in the playroom and in a few moments came out carrying a little bell with a wooden handle.

When they reached the tower, Bert tied the bell to the bananas with a piece of string from his pocket. Then he moved the empty hatbox to the middle of the floor and placed the fruit on it.

"We'll have to keep watch all night for Milly," said Chuck.

"We can take turns sitting on the steps," suggested Flossie.

"Mother will never let us do that," said Patti. "We'll have to stay awake in our beds."

"I hope nobody falls asleep," Freddie remarked. "Milly could sneak in, take the bananas and get away again."

"Don't worry about that," said Bert. "We'll be sure to hear the bell."

Nan nodded. "We can leave the trapdoor open and also the door at the foot of the stairs."

The children told Mrs. Parker what they planned to do and she approved the idea. Later they went down and kept watch at the schoolhouse, but there was no sign of the spook.

"I'm tired of this," Flossie complained. "Let's go for a swim."

"Okay," said Nan.

They splashed and swam for some time. Then Freddie climbed out and called Flossie aside. He whispered to her for a moment, and the two children put on their robes and slippers and headed for the house.

"Where are you going?" Chuck called.

"We'll be back in a minute," Freddie answered over his shoulder. "We have to fix something."

"It's a secret," Flossie added.

That night the boys took first watch. By twelve o'clock, Freddie was asleep but Chuck and Bert were wide awake with the lamp on.

Suddenly Bert said, "Listen!"

Both boys pricked up their ears. They had heard the bell!

Quickly they dashed toward the stairs to the tower.

"Shh!" Bert warned. "Don't scare her!"

He started on tiptoe up the steps with Chuck at his heels. Suddenly something big and dark came clattering down the stairway toward them!

"Look out!" cried Chuck.

CHAPTER VIII

THE MYSTERIOUS KEYCASE

THE two boys flattened themselves against the wall. A big ball clattered noisily down the stairs past them and out into the hall.

"What was that?" Chuck asked fearfully.

Bert was already running up the tower stairs. As he climbed through the open trapdoor he gave a disappointed exclamation. The moonlit room was empty. The bananas, hatbox and bell were gone!

"We're too late!" he said, as Chuck came up behind him. "Milly must have been here and taken them."

"I guess all that noise scared her away," Chuck remarked.

"Maybe she's still on the roof," said Bert, heading for the open window.

At the same time Mr. Parker called from below and the girls' voices could be heard also. Chuck hurried down to explain to them.

Bert climbed over the sill onto the almost flat roof. Walking around the tower, he could see the gray slates gleaming in the moonlight. He circled the tall chimney. There was no sign of the monkey.

Moments later Chuck, Nan and Patti climbed out the window, followed by Mr. Parker.

"Milly!" the girls called anxiously.

"Shh! Listen!" said Bert. From somewhere below came the tinkling of a bell. The five moved cautiously to the roof edge and saw a tiny figure, carrying a hatbox by the string, disappear into the orchard.

"Milly! Come back!" Patti cried. But the ringing grew fainter in the night.

"I'm afraid it's no use following her," said Mr. Parker. "We'd never catch up. She has too much of a head start."

"I never thought she'd take the box and all," said Bert.

"It's very light and she can swing it by the cord," said Patti. "She likes to play with things like that." Her eyes filled with tears.

"Don't worry," said Nan kindly. "We'll catch Milly somehow."

The children and Mr. Parker climbed back into the tower and went downstairs. The light was on in the hall now. The young twins were waiting with Mrs. Parker in robes and slippers. At their feet was a giant beach ball tied to a roller skate.

"No wonder that made so much noise!" exclaimed Chuck. "Who rigged this up?"

Bert eyed his little brother and sister. They looked sheepish.

"It was my idea," said Freddie in a small voice. "I was afraid that whoever was on watch would fall asleep, so we tied the ball to the skate and put it at the edge of the trapdoor. I figured if Milly came she'd knock the ball down the stairs, and everyone would hear it and wake up."

"We thought we were helping," piped up Flossie.

Bert looked sternly at the young twins. "Well, your plan backfired."

"Never mind," said Mrs. Parker, patting Freddie's and Flossie's shoulders. "You meant well."

Sadly the two children took the contraption apart and returned the toys to the playroom.

In the morning the Bobbsey boys were awake before Chuck. "I think we left the trapdoor open last night," said Bert softly. "I'd better close it."

"I'll help you," said Freddie, hoping to make up for his mistake of the day before.

The two boys slipped quietly into jeans and T-shirts, then went up to the tower. Before closing the trapdoor, they decided to check the little room for clues.

In a few minutes Freddie spotted something

between two boxes. He picked it up. "Look! A keycase!"

Bert took the black leather object and examined it. "That's funny. It wasn't up here yesterday morning."

"Is there a name on it?" Freddie asked.

"No, just the initial S on the front," Bert observed. "Good work, Freddie," he added and tucked the case into his pocket. The brothers left the tower room, closing the trapdoor behind them.

At breakfast Bert told what Freddie had found and passed the keycase around the table.

"It doesn't belong to any of us Parkers," said Chuck.

Nan's eyes grew wide. "I have an idea! You know how Milly is always picking up things? Well, maybe whoever took her left the keycase lying around and she grabbed it."

"And dropped it in the tower room last night," Patti added excitedly.

Everyone agreed this was probably what had happened.

"Mr. Parker," said Bert, laying down his fork, "why don't you put an ad in the Lost-and-Found section of your paper telling that the keycase has been found, but don't say where. Whoever comes for it might be the person who captured Milly."

"Good idea! We'll try that," said Mr. Parker,

taking another piece of toast. "But just remember, Milly could have picked it up anywhere. It might not really belong to the 'spook.'" As he buttered his toast, the newspaperman smiled. "What are your plans for your other case—the canalboat treasure?"

"I've been thinking about it," said Nan. "Maybe your Aunt Emily put it away in a chest or a dresser."

"No, we've looked through all her personal things," said Mrs. Parker. "She had nothing from canal days."

"Maybe the captain hid it in the house somewhere," Bert suggested.

"That could be," said Mrs. Parker. "Why don't you search the unused rooms on the top floor? You'll find lots of old boxes and trunks up there that we haven't had time to examine."

"It'll take a long while to search all of them," Nan said.

"I know what!" Freddie spoke up. "We could ask the Pet Club to help!"

"Would that be all right, Mother?" asked Patti.

"If you put everything back as you found it."

An hour later the club members had gathered on the front porch of the Parkers' house.

"What's it all about?" Sally asked. "Did you find Milly?"

"Not exactly," said Bert.

As he reported the monkey's nighttime visit, the children listened in amazement. When Nan explained about the search for the captain's treasure, they were even more excited.

"That'll be fun!" said Bill Dugan.

All morning the children hunted carefully. They looked in closets, cartons and trunks, but found nothing that could have been the missing treasure.

Dusty and tired, the children gathered again on the porch. Nan, Patti and Flossie served lemonade and cookies.

Bill Dugan announced that the club would come at seven that evening to his house. "My mother said we could have the meetings in our rumpus room until the mystery is solved."

After lunch the six cousins went down to the schoolhouse. As they walked into the classroom, Freddie gave a surprised shout. He saw the hatbox in a corner!

"How did that get in here?" Patti asked.

"Maybe Milly brought it," said Bert. "She could have come in through the belfry, you know."

"Maybe she's here now," said Nan. But they found no sign of the monkey.

Leaving the empty box, they went outside and kept watch. Nothing happened, so they decided to go swimming for the rest of the afternoon.

After supper they started for the meeting with Cooky trotting behind. At Bill's house

"Will the club meeting please come to order!"
the president said

Mrs. Dugan directed them to a big room in the basement. It was furnished with bright orange and black couches and chairs. Most of the other children were there with their pets. When everyone had arrived, Bill called out, "Will the meeting please come to order?" Everyone sat down on the floor.

"Dick Wood will give us a report on feeding turtles."

Suddenly Fritzi started barking at the open window above a couch. "Stop it, Fritzi! Lie down!" Sally said. But the little dog would not stop.

"There are some stray cats around," Bill said. "I guess that's what he hears." Finally Fritzi lay down.

When the turtle report was over, Chuck spoke up. "I keep thinking about that canalboat treasure. What could it be?"

Most of the children had no idea. "We don't even know if it's big or little," said Flossie.

"I'll bet it was money or jewels belonging to the passengers," said Bill loudly. "The captain probably kept the stuff in a big strongbox."

"You could be right," Nan murmured.

As she spoke Fritzi growled again, but Sally ordered him to be quiet. The children went on talking about the *Erie Belle* and the missing treasure for a while. Then the meeting was adjourned.

"I'm going to get an ice cream cone before I

go home," said Chuck. "Anybody want to come with me?"

"I do!" said Freddie and Flossie together.

"Not me," said Bert. "I think I'll go by way of the towpath and check on the schoolhouse."

A few minutes later everyone started home. It was almost dark as the older twins and Patti walked down through Bill's back yard and along the canal. Now and then they heard the plop of a frog among the reeds.

Suddenly there was a loud crackle in the bushes nearby. They stopped and listened.

"Who's there?" Bert called. No answer.

"Probably just a rabbit," said Nan. But she remembered how excited Fritzi had been at the meeting. Had someone been spying on them? Was he watching them now?

By the time the children neared the schoolhouse, it was dark. When they rounded the bend, Nan gave a sharp gasp.

"Look!" She pointed ahead. There was a wavering light inside the building. "The spook must be in there!"

Cautiously the three children walked up and peered in the window. A candle was burning on the teacher's desk! But the room was empty!

Quickly they went to the front of the school. Bert took his pencil flashlight from his pocket and shone it through a small window at the end of the cloakroom. They could see no one inside!

"Oh, it's scary!" Patti said with a shiver.

"I'm going in," said Bert.

"I'll go with you," Nan offered.

"I will, too," whispered Patti. "I don't want to stay out here by myself."

The children tiptoed to the front door. It was locked, so Patti used her key. As they stepped inside, Bert's flashlight beam wavered and went out.

"Oh, no!" he muttered.

Softly the three walked to the left door and looked into the classroom. The candle cast a weird, flickering light over the empty desks and the blank blackboard. Bert started forward cautiously with the girls right behind him.

Just then they heard a noise in the cloakroom. They stopped short and listened. In a few seconds they tiptoed back to the door and looked into the anteroom. As their eyes became accustomed to the dark, they saw no one there.

"Maybe it was a mouse," said Bert quietly. As the children turned back into the classroom, Patti cried out in fright. In front of the blackboard was a glowing figure!

CHAPTER IX

ROOFTOP SURPRISE

FOR a moment the children froze in terror. Then Bert looked hard at the weird figure glowing against the blackboard.

"It's a drawing!" he exclaimed.

"Why, so it is!" said Nan, taking a second look.

Patti peered through the candlelit gloom. "It's still scary," she whispered.

Bert led the way down the aisle and up onto the platform. He rubbed his finger across the scowling white face of the "ghost."

"I thought so! Glowing chalk!" he said.

"But I don't understand it!" said Nan. "A minute ago there wasn't anything on the board, and now here's this drawing!"

"It just isn't possible!" said Patti.

Puzzled, the children looked around the empty room. Their eyes went to the teacher's desk, with the single candle burning on it. Some-

"It's scary!" said Patti. "Let's get out of here!"

one must be hiding under it! Bert's heart pounded as he went over and peeked underneath.

"Nobody there," he said.

"But who lit that candle and drew the picture?" Nan asked.

Bert shook his head, puzzled. "My guess is that someone spied on the club meeting, heard our plans and beat us here. You remember how Fritzi barked and the noise we heard in the bushes?"

"Yes," said Nan, "but no human being could have drawn the picture that fast and then disappeared!"

"It's all too scary!" said Patti. "Let's get out of here!"

Bert examined the candle but found nothing unusual. He used it to light their way out of the schoolhouse.

Patti locked the door and Bert led the way up the dark wooded hill, carrying the candle. At every noise they stopped to listen.

"I hope the spook isn't after us," Patti whispered.

When they saw the welcome lights of the house, the trio began to run and burst into the kitchen. The younger children and Mrs. Parker were there, working on a picture puzzle.

"Mother, we saw a spook!" cried Patti. Excitedly she told what had happened.

Mrs. Parker looked worried. "We'll tell

Daddy when he comes home," she said, and explained that her husband was at a town meeting making plans for the Cherry Festival. "He won't be back until late."

"Ooo!" exclaimed Flossie. "I'll never go to that clubhouse by myself!"

Early the next morning the whole family trooped down the hill together. Patti unlocked the schoolhouse door and everyone hurried into the classroom. The drawing was gone!

"The blackboard's been washed clean," Mr. Parker remarked. "Somebody came back and removed all evidence of the trick."

"And I wanted to see the funny picture," said Freddie.

"I wish I knew how it was done," said Nan.

"There had to be at least two people here," said Bert. "One made the noise in the cloakroom to draw us away while the other worked the spook trick."

Freddie had been trying to find a little of the glowing chalk dust. As he stooped down below the blackboard he noticed a small hole in the platform about as big as a dime. The little boy stuck his finger in, then drew it out again.

"Maybe the ghost went through there," he said, laughing.

Bert grinned. "I think that's too small even for a spook, Freddie. There must be a secret entrance somewhere," he added. "Let's try to find it."

They all looked carefully in every part of the schoolhouse but could not find a hidden opening.

Mr. Parker said, "These mischief-makers must have a duplicate key, so we'll add a new lock."

He took tools and a padlock kit from his pocket and attached the hasps to the door and snapped the padlock in place.

"Here's a key," he said, giving it to Patti. "But I don't like what's going on down here," he added. "None of you must ever come here alone."

He and his wife returned to the house, but the children stayed to search for clues. Bert pulled a magnifying glass from his pocket to search for footprints, but there were too many to distinguish one from another. Finally the children went back up the hill.

As they entered the house, Mr. Parker called to them from the living room. The six went in. A large man in a gray suit was seated on the sofa. He had thick black hair and a huge mustache which covered his upper lip.

Mr. Parker introduced the children, then said, "This is Mr. Louis Burden. He's president of the Burden Amusement Company in Albany." The cousins greeted the visitor politely.

He smiled, showing unusually large white teeth. "We put on carnivals, shows, circuses, and magic acts—you just name it, we have it!"

"Mr. Burden and his two brothers would like to buy our schoolhouse," said Mr. Parker. "They're opening a tourist attraction upstate called 'Yesterday Village.' It will show things as they were in a small New York town a hundred years ago."

"We would like to have an authentic old schoolhouse," explained the big man.

Mr. Parker smiled. "Mr. Burden was here before, but I told him that the place was not for sale because you were using it. Now I don't know." He looked questioningly at the children. "Do you still want it for your club?"

"Oh, yes!" said Patti quickly.

"It's not always going to be haunted," added Chuck positively. "I'm sure the Bobbseys will catch the spook."

Mr. Parker smiled and turned to Mr. Burden. "I'm afraid the answer is still no."

The big man scowled and heaved himself to his feet. "I'm sorry to hear it," he said, "but if you change your mind, let me know." Then he shook hands with Mr. Parker, who walked with him toward the front door. The children said good-by, but he did not answer.

When the two men had left the room, Flossie said softly, "I don't think I like Mr. Burden, 'cause he isn't very friendly."

Patti smiled. "He certainly has the biggest walrus mustache I ever saw."

Flossie giggled. "We could call him Mr. Walrus."

Meanwhile, Bert had been watching from the window as the visitor got into his black car and drove away.

"I've been thinking," said Bert seriously when Mr. Parker came back. "Do you suppose that the Burden brothers could be trying to scare us out of the schoolhouse?"

"That's an idea!" Patti exclaimed. "The haunting started about two weeks ago. When did Mr. Burden first come here, Daddy?"

"A few days before that," her father replied. "The idea occurred to me too, but I counted it out. You see, the Burdens are known as very fine men. Every year they give many free shows for needy children. I feel sure that people like that would not try to frighten you."

"I see what you mean," said Bert.

That afternoon the boys took Cooky and walked down to Bill's house to tell him about the glowing spook. Afterward they went fishing in the canal. At the same time, the girls visited Mr. O'Neal, hoping to varnish some more toys.

"I'm especially glad to see you today, young ladies," said the little carpenter, " 'cause I can use help. Mike's away on a trip." Mr. O'Neal gave all the children big aprons to put over their shorts and shirts.

"Did you finish the canalboat you were working on?" Flossie asked as she settled down at the workbench.

Mr. O'Neal pointed to a shelf where the model craft stood brightly painted in yellow and red. "There she is! And I wish she were a full-size boat."

Suddenly Nan's eyes sparkled. "Why don't you make a big one?" she asked. "Then you could give tourists rides on the canal."

"Wouldn't I like to!" exclaimed Mr. O'Neal. "I even drew up plans for a big packet last year, but the Town Council said it would cost too much. Cherry Corners could never afford it!"

"That's too bad," said Nan. "I think lots of people would come to ride on it."

"Yes," said the carpenter. "Mike and I are all ready to go ahead with it. If the town ever gets the money we could build it in short order!"

While Flossie carefully varnished a tray of little dogs and cats, the older girls painted wooden cherries bright red with green leaves.

When they finished, Mr. O'Neal praised them and gave them cookies with soda. As they left, he called, "Thanks for coming!"

That evening Mrs. Parker suggested that everyone go to the band concert in the park. As soon as it was dark they started. The children walked ahead with Cooky.

At the end of Main Street they entered a small park. In the middle of it stood a brightly lit bandstand. The musicians wore red uniforms with gold trimmings and played shiny brass instruments.

"They're bee-yoo-ti-ful!" Flossie said, clapping.

While Mr. and Mrs. Parker sat on a bench to listen to the loud, gay music, the children walked around among the trees. Cooky ran off with some other dogs.

During a lively piece Freddie and Flossie began to march along to the music. When it was over, they stopped near a high clump of bushes.

After the loud applause there was a pause. In the sudden quiet the twins heard a man say in a deep voice, "Now he wants us to look for some kind of canalboat treasure!"

"He's the boss," replied another man. His voice was high and thin. "We have to follow orders."

"Maybe they're talking about our treasure!" Freddie whispered excitedly to his twin.

Flossie grabbed his hand and they slipped around the bushes. They saw a crowd of people moving toward a refreshment stand.

"There are lots of men," said Flossie, disappointed. "We can't tell which two were talking."

The young twins found the older children and reported what they had heard.

Bert looked grim. "Whoever spied on our club meeting probably heard us speak about the treasure. Now he and his pals are looking for it."

When the concert was over, the children told Mr. and Mrs. Parker what had happened.

"Now we know one thing definite," said Mr. Parker. "There are at least three men in the spook business."

As the family was leaving the park, Patti's mother and father lingered to talk to a friend. The children trotted ahead, expecting Cooky to follow.

When they neared home, Nan suddenly said, "Wait! Look!" She pointed to the house. In the moonlight they could see the trellis shaking.

"What makes it do that?" asked Freddie. "I don't see anybody on it!"

"I think I saw something dark moving onto the roof," said Bert.

"Maybe it's Milly!" exclaimed Patti.

"Give me your key, quick!" said Bert. "I'll go up to the roof. Freddie, run and tell Mr. Parker. The rest of you stay at the bottom of the trellis!"

Patti handed him the key and Bert dashed off. Moments later he was taking two steps at a time to the tower. Quietly he opened the trapdoor. There was not a sound.

Bert peered into the small room. In the moonlight he could see it was empty.

Quickly he slipped through the open window onto the roof. He heard a soft noise.

"That came from behind the chimney," he thought, and walked quietly across the slates toward it.

"Milly!" he called softly. "Don't be afraid!"

As he spoke, Bert rounded the chimney. He froze in his tracks! Before him crouched a huge man with a black bag over his head!

CHAPTER X

THE RUNAWAY

THE masked man clapped a hand over Bert's mouth. "Don't make a sound or you'll be sorry," he said harshly.

The next moment he dashed across the roof to the trellis. Swiftly he began to climb down.

Despite the warning, Bert ran to the edge and called to the children below, "Stop him!"

Halfway down, the man swung himself around the big clump of wisteria and disappeared below it.

"Here he comes!" cried Nan, pointing up while the others screamed for Mr. Parker.

"Get ready to jump on him!" cried Chuck as he and the three girls clustered anxiously around the foot of the trellis.

But all at once the man leaped free, clear over their heads and fell to the ground. Bounding to his feet, he dashed off before they could stop him.

Mr. Parker raced up with Freddie. "What's the matter?"

By this time Bert came running from the house. "Catch that man!" he shouted.

He led the chase across the moonlit back yard and down into the dark orchard. The man vanished among the trees.

"No use," said Bert, panting to a stop. "We've lost him."

The searchers walked back to the house.

"I'll bet," said Nan, "that he's one of the spooks and was looking for the canalboat treasure." The others agreed.

Mr. Parker went at once to the telephone and called the police. A few minutes later two officers arrived in a patrol car. After hearing Bert's story, they looked around the tower room and the roof. There were no clues.

"I doubt if this fellow got into the house," said the policeman. "He probably heard you children talking below and stayed hidden on the roof."

Meanwhile the Parkers had been checking through the rooms. They reported that nothing valuable was missing. With their large flashlight, the two officers examined the ground around the trellis, but there were too many footprints for any of them to be clear.

As the police left, Cooky came trotting up the porch steps. Nan let him in. "You're too late, Cooky," she said. "The prowler is gone."

The next day was Sunday. After church the older twins went to the tower with their cousins. They wanted to look for clues which the police might have missed.

The dust in the middle of the floor had been disturbed by the people coming and going in the room. But in one untouched corner, Nan noticed a round clean spot in the thick grayness. She stood looking at it thoughtfully.

"What's the matter?" Patti asked.

"I never noticed that place before," Nan said. "It looks as if something used to stand there."

"Maybe it was the missing treasure," Bert suggested. "Perhaps the prowler took it."

Nan nodded. "Or Milly. We know how she likes to pick up things and carry them around."

The children stared at the spot. It was about three inches wide. "It was something round on the bottom," Nan said. "What could it be?"

"Who knows?" said Chuck, shrugging.

Patti sighed. "I really don't care what the treasure is or where it is. All I want is to find Milly."

As the four went downstairs, delicious odors drew them to the kitchen. They found Mrs. Parker preparing a roast beef dinner. Flossie was whipping cream with the electric beater while Freddie mashed strawberries for the shortcake.

"That looks cool!" exclaimed Bert. Then he reported what they had seen in the tower.

Nan added, "If Milly did carry some small round thing away, I think it must be made of metal." She explained that the tapping she had heard at the window a few nights before had sounded like metal hitting glass.

"That seems reasonable," said Mrs. Parker, "but I can't imagine what the thing could have been."

In midafternoon the older girls and Bert decided to go for a dip in the back yard pool. This time Flossie did not want to go. She had been thinking about the riding stable. She told her twin and Chuck that Mr. Brewster had invited her to have a look around.

"That's a great idea," said Freddie.

"Let's go," said Chuck. "Maybe we can feed the horses."

Ten minutes later when they arrived, there was a black two-wheeled carriage standing in the street. Hitched to it was a sleek white horse. Mr. Brewster was placing a large garland of red paper flowers around the horse's neck.

"Hello, Mr. Brewster," said Flossie. "Why are you doing that?"

"Just trying on Betsy's costume," he said, smiling. "During Cherry Festival time I give rides in this old carriage. Then the horse and reins and even the wheels are twined with wreaths of paper flowers."

"Where are the other flowers?" Freddie asked.

"I'm going inside now to get them," he said.

As Mr. Brewster went back into the building, the children saw Danny Rugg coming across the street. "What is this old thing?" he asked, kicking one of the carriage wheels.

"What's it look like?" Freddie asked.

Danny stuck his hand in his pocket. "I'll bet you kids are afraid of that horse."

"I am not!" declared Freddie.

"We are not!" said Flossie and Chuck together.

"Then I dare you to climb up and take the reins," said Danny.

"I don't think the man would want us to," said Freddie.

Danny laughed. "Chicken! That's you!" he taunted. "Three chickens!"

"We are not!" declared Chuck angrily.

"Afraid of a plain old everyday horse!" sneered Danny. "Wait'll I tell the kids back home!"

Red-faced, Freddie promptly climbed up into the driver's seat and Chuck scrambled up behind him. Flossie followed quickly.

"See, Danny!" cried Freddie as he reached for the reins.

At that moment Danny hit the horse hard on the flank. "Giddap!" he yelled.

The animal bolted down the street. Frightened, Freddie tried to catch the reins, but they

"Whoa!" Freddie cried. "Help!"

had fallen down. "Whoa!" he cried. "Help!"

The horse sped straight down Main Street, dodging a few automobiles. The children clung screaming to the seats. A policeman heard them.

He dashed out and caught the animal by the bridle. In a few moments he managed to bring the runaway to a stop. "Oh, Officer Wright, thank you," said Chuck.

"Why are you children in this carriage?" he asked sternly.

Shakily Chuck explained. The young twins were trembling with fright.

"You should not have taken the dare," said the officer. He helped them down, then led the horse and carriage back to the riding stable. The children followed.

Mr. Brewster was there, holding Danny firmly by the arm. "I saw what happened," he said. "Someone could have been badly hurt."

"We're very sorry," quavered Freddie.

"This Rugg boy is going to be sorry too," said the policeman. He scolded the bully so sharply that Danny grew red and hung his head.

"Now come along," Officer Wright told him. "I'm taking you to your mother."

As he led Danny away, the young twins and Chuck apologized to Mr. Brewster and said good-by.

When they reached home, Freddie sheepishly told what had happened.

"You were lucky you weren't hurt," said Nan.

"I wouldn't want to be Danny now." Bert grinned. "He's in for it!"

That night, before going to bed, the cousins decided to take turns watching the newspaper office the next day.

"Maybe somebody will come for the keycase," said Nan hopefully.

In the morning as the children were going out the door, the telephone rang. Patti stopped to answer it. While she listened, her face fell. The others waited curiously.

"Okay, Daddy. Thanks for calling," she said and hung up.

"What's the matter?" Chuck asked.

"We're too late. A man came for the keycase a few minutes ago. He said he had lost it while walking on the canal bank. His name was Smith."

The children exclaimed excitedly and Bert asked, "What did he look like?"

"He was tall, and wore big sunglasses and a straw hat."

"Did Daddy talk to him?" asked Chuck.

"No, it happened before he got there. The secretary in the front office was supposed to delay the person until Daddy could see him, but she was away from her desk. The office boy didn't know about it and handed over the case."

Bert frowned. "Too bad."

"I wish we'd get some good news," said Freddie.

Nan spoke up. "I know something that would cheer us up. Let's go to Mr. O'Neal's place. Some of those little animals should be dry. Maybe we could each buy one."

Ten minutes later the children came to the carpenter's shop and went in.

"We'd like to buy some of those little animals, Mr. O'Neal," said Nan.

He stood up, wiped his hands on a gray apron which almost went to the floor and frowned at them. "You would, would you? Well, those creatures are not for sale."

The children's faces showed their disappointment. But the little carpenter gave a great big smile. "They're not for sale to *you*, of course! You helped to make them. Just pick out what you want and consider it a present."

"Oh, how nice!" exclaimed Nan.

"Thank you!" the other children chimed in happily.

"Not at all, not at all," said Mr. O'Neal, waving toward the rows of little carvings on the workbench. "I intended to give each of you something. Just march over and take your pick."

Freddie and Flossie each chose a dog. Nan and Patti took bunches of cherries while Bert picked an elephant, and Chuck a giraffe.

Mr. O'Neal put each toy into a little brown

bag. After thanking him again, the cousins said good-by. As they went out the door Mike O'Neal pulled up in his dark blue sedan.

"Patti Parker!" he called out the window. "You're just the girl I want to see. I have news for you!"

CHAPTER XI

"WATCH OUT BELOW!"

"WHAT'S the news?" Patti asked eagerly as Mike swung out of the driver's seat.

"I think I saw your monkey," said the tall young man.

"Oh, where?" cried Patti.

"Up north of here—in Rochester," said Mike. "It was yesterday evening. I was pulling into a gas station when a young woman in a red convertible drove out. She had a monkey on the seat beside her. The little fellow had something yellow on, a sweater, I think."

"Oh, I'm sure it was Milly!" exclaimed Flossie.

Mike went on, "I honked the horn at the lady, but she didn't stop. Then I asked the gas station attendant if he knew anything about her. He said, 'She's a tourist. Wanted to know how to get to Watkins Glen. The lady had several places to go first but hoped to arrive at the glen tonight.'"

"Maybe Mother could drive us there this afternoon," Chuck said eagerly.

"That's a great idea!" Patti replied. "Let's ask her."

After thanking Mike for the information, the cousins raced down the street. When they reached home Patti poured out the story to Mrs. Parker.

"We'll head for Watkins Glen right after lunch," she said, slipping off her apron. "I've been meaning to take you children on a little trip around New York State anyway."

Flossie spoke up. "Do you think the lady is one of the spooks?"

"We'll find out," Nan replied, "when we learn how she got the monkey."

While the girls made sandwiches and poured milk for lunch, Mrs. Parker called her husband and told him about the trip.

After eating, the children packed bags and changed into fresh clothes. Then Bert telephoned Bill. He explained where they were going and why.

"Okay," said the club president. "I'll keep an eye on the schoolhouse."

"Be careful," Bert warned. "You'd better not go there alone."

"Don't worry," Bill promised. "No old spook's going to get me! Good luck in finding Milly," he added.

A few minutes later Mrs. Parker and the children piled into the station wagon. Cooky stood on the lawn and barked as Mrs. Parker backed the car out of the driveway.

"Be good, Cooky!" Flossie called, "and watch out for spooks!"

As the station wagon rolled along the highway, the children gazed out the windows at the wide green farms.

Suddenly Patti said, "Mother! I almost forgot! Do you think we'll be back in time for my birthday?"

Mrs. Parker smiled. "If we find Milly tonight, we can be home again by tomorrow. But I thought it would be fun to go on to Cooperstown and then take a ride on the Erie Canal. We'll be gone no longer than three days."

"That's in plenty of time for your party, Patti," said Chuck. "Your birthday isn't till Saturday—five days from now."

It was evening when the family drove into the small town of Watkins Glen. "It's too late to visit the glen now," said Mrs. Parker. "We'll go first thing in the morning."

She pulled up in front of a motel on the shore of a big blue lake. "This is Seneca Lake," she said.

"There was an Indian tribe by that name, too," Bert spoke up. "Lots of them lived in this territory before the Revolutionary War."

After a hearty supper in the motel, the cousins took a walk along the shore until it was dark. "I never saw such a long lake before," said Flossie.

"This is one of the Finger Lakes," Chuck told her. "There are eleven of them in New York and they're all long and narrow like fingers on a hand. That's how they got their name."

Upon returning to the motel the children looked over the cars, but there was no red convertible among them.

"The lady is probably staying at some other motel," Bert said.

In the morning Mrs. Parker checked out and drove the children to a parking lot at the foot of the glen. Straight ahead they saw the high rocky walls of the chasm. A stream flowed down between them and splashed into a pool. At one side of the lot stood a red convertible. It was empty.

"That may be the car," said Nan.

"The woman must be in the glen already," said Bert. "I wonder if she has the monkey with her."

"This is the bottom entrance," Mrs. Parker said. "I suggest that you children take a taxi to the top and start walking down along the pathway. Here, Bert, take some money. I'll wait here in the car. Whether the woman is going up the canyon from the bottom or coming down from the top, between us we ought to catch her."

"Let's go!" Bert urged.

The children got out of the station wagon and hurried over to a car marked *Glen Top Taxi*.

"Hop in," said the driver cheerfully. Patti and Nan sat on the jump seats, while the other four squeezed into the back seat.

The car started with a lurch and went up a winding road. Soon it stopped in a parking lot on top of the hill.

As Bert paid the man, the others got out. They saw arrow signs on trees pointing to the glen. Straight ahead was a refreshment and souvenir store.

"Oh, let's go in there first," said Freddie.

"All right," Nan agreed, "but make it quick."

The young twins ran into the shop. In a few minutes they came out, each wearing a pointed green hat with a long feather on it.

"Those are cute," said Nan.

The children followed the arrows to the edge of the glen. It was a deep, narrow chasm with a sparkling stream at the bottom. No one was in sight.

Carefully they started down the path, single file, gazing at the craggy sides with trees growing out of them. Along the outer edge of the trail was a low stone wall.

After a while they passed under a natural rock arch and came out again close to a waterfall. Tiny droplets of the splashing water blew in their faces.

"Oh, feel the spray!" exclaimed Flossie. As the others kept walking downward, she lingered

"My hat!" cried Flossie

behind to look over the wall. A sudden sharp breeze blew her hat off!

"Help! My hat!" she cried. The others turned to see the green cone with the long feather blowing down the glen. It lighted on the fast-moving water and bobbed along merrily.

"I'll get it for you!" cried a voice.

Some distance below them on the trail was a boy wearing a hat like Flossie's. He had a long souvenir cane in his hand. Where he was standing, the path was low and very close to the water.

"Don't worry, I'll hook it!" he called, brandishing the cane.

The others hurried toward the boy. Freddie was so excited he began to run.

"Stop!" cried Nan. "It's too steep!"

Freddie tried to slow down, but he was going too fast.

"Look out below!" he yelled in a frightened voice. "I can't stop!"

As the boy with the cane turned in surprise, Freddie ran straight into him. With a grunt the older boy plopped down on the path and Freddie fell on top of him. Their hats flew off into the water.

"Are you hurt?" Nan asked anxiously as the others gathered around and helped the two boys to their feet.

"No," said the stranger breathlessly, as his hand went to his head, "but our hats are gone."

Freddie looked sheepish. "I'm sorry. I didn't mean to bump into you."

The children looked down on the stream. Freddie grinned in spite of himself. The three hats were bobbing along together, their feathers blowing in the wind.

"They look funny!" Flossie said, and giggled.

"Where are you from?" asked the boy, who was about Bert's age. He was short with black hair and a friendly smile.

"We're from Lakeport," Bert said. He explained about visiting Cherry Corners and introduced everyone.

The boy replied that he was Benny Brown from Troy, New York.

"We're looking for somebody," Nan said and told about the woman with the monkey in the yellow sweater.

The boy's eyes grew wide with interest. "I haven't seen her," he said. "She must be somewhere ahead of me."

As they walked along together, the stream fell away and was once again a good distance beneath them. Suddenly Chuck pointed to a crevice in the rocks below.

"There's something yellow sticking out!" he exclaimed. "Maybe that's Milly!"

Patti clapped her hands. "Oh, I hope so, but how will we ever get her out?"

"That crack is too far down for us to reach,"

Nan said as they all looked over the low wall.

"I could do it with your cane, Benny," Bert said. "Would you mind lending it to me?"

"Course not! That's a good idea."

Patti spoke up. "If Milly's in there, maybe she'll take hold of the handle and you can pull her up."

Bert took the cane from the boy and leaned over the parapet. The curved end reached just to the crevice in the rock wall.

"Milly!" Patti called down. "Come on out, Milly!"

But no small brown head appeared.

CHAPTER XII

THE TWINS IN TROUBLE

"I guess Milly's not in there," said Bert, poking at the yellow cloth with the cane.

"Maybe it's just her sweater," Nan suggested. "But how did it get into that crevice?"

Patti looked worried as she peered at the rocky wall of the cliff. "Milly might have climbed down to the crack and taken off her sweater there."

"Hold on!" Bert exclaimed. "I've caught it!"

Carefully he pulled the yellow material from the crevice and began to bring it up on the hook of the cane.

"Oh, it's only a scarf!" Nan exclaimed.

"I'm glad!" said Patti. "I was afraid Milly had fallen into the stream."

"What'll we do with this?" asked Chuck, taking the scarf off the end of the cane.

"Leave it on these rocks beside the path," said

Benny. "Maybe the person who lost it will come back for it."

Chuck put it down and Patti placed a stone on top. "So it can't blow away," she explained.

"We'd better hurry," said Bert, "if we want to catch up with the woman who has the monkey."

"I guess you'd better," Benny agreed. "I wish you luck!"

The children thanked him and, calling good-by, hurried down the path toward the bottom of the glen. Although they walked quickly, the searchers did not see the woman ahead of them.

"She has to come to the bottom," Nan said. "Your mother will be sure to catch her there."

But when the children came out into the parking lot the red convertible was gone. And so were Mrs. Parker and the station wagon!

"Where can she be?" Patti asked. Puzzled, the children stood to one side, waiting.

Suddenly Nan cried, "Here she comes!" The big brown station wagon was turning into the lot.

"Where were you? What happened?" Patti asked her mother as the car pulled up.

"Did you see the monkey?" Chuck put in.

"One at a time!" said Mrs. Parker, shaking her head. "Yes, I saw the woman with the monkey. As she came out of the glen, I got out of the car and hurried toward her, but the next moment she had slid into her convertible. I called to her, but she didn't wait, just drove off."

"So you got in the car and chased her," Bert added.

Mrs. Parker nodded. "Yes, but I lost her out on the highway. I'm sorry, children," she said. "I know how disappointed you are."

Patti was trying not to cry. "Did you see Milly?"

"I saw a little woolly monkey wearing a yellow sweater," said her mother. "It could have been Milly."

"What did the woman look like?" Nan asked.

"She had short blond hair and wore a blue slack suit."

"We know she's a tourist," Bert said. "Maybe she went on to Cooperstown."

"That could be," said Mrs. Parker. "We'll head there at once."

It was midafternoon when the group arrived at Cooperstown. Mrs. Parker parked on the main street. As the travelers walked a short distance to the Hall of Fame, they saw no sign of the red car.

They entered the brick building and filed around looking at the bronze plaques which commemorated famous baseball players. They saw trophies, pictures and old baseball equipment. But nowhere did they spot the woman with the monkey.

"We'll try the Carriage and Harness Museum," Mrs. Parker said.

A few minutes later they entered the nearby building. In a room with dark wooden walls, they saw three tall men looking at an old buggy.

"There's the circus man!" Flossie whispered, tugging at Nan's sleeve.

"You're right," her sister said quietly, and told the rest of the children. "Maybe the other men are his brothers."

At that moment Mr. Burden looked up. For a second he stared blankly at the children, then a great white-toothed smile spread across his face. He nodded to them and Mrs. Parker. The children smiled back politely and watched the three men walk into the adjoining room.

"I wonder what they're doing here," Bert said.

"Probably looking over the buggies to see what they would like to have in their old-time village," said Nan.

For a few minutes the family wandered around together, enjoying the exhibits. Then the children drifted into the next room.

"Oh, see the horses!" exclaimed Freddie.

Straight ahead were two life-sized models of horses hitched to a wagon.

"They're white as snow!" Nan remarked.

A thin man in a guard's uniform came around the side of the wagon. His long, bony face was grim.

"Oh, we didn't do it!" Nan exclaimed

"Anybody in here named Bobbsey?" he asked loudly.

Startled, the twins looked up as several other visitors turned around curiously.

"That's our name," Bert said.

The man's eyes narrowed. "Oh, it is, is it?" He beckoned to the twins. "Come around here, please."

All the children followed the guard to the other side of the horses. Printed on one of them in blue chalk were the words: THE BOBB-SEYS WROTE THIS.

"Oh, we didn't do that!" Nan exclaimed. "None of us wrote on that horse!"

"Of course not!" Bert declared as the other children chimed in.

The guard gave them a long, hard look. "Anybody else around here know you?" he asked.

Just then Mrs. Parker came in. "What's the matter?" she asked, coming up to the group.

As she saw the words written on the side of the horse, her eyes sparkled angrily. "I'm sure that these children did not do that," she said firmly to the guard. "This is some kind of a trick."

"If we *had* done it," Bert spoke up, "we wouldn't have admitted that we were the Bobbseys."

"That's true," the guard agreed. "You don't look like the kind who would do something like this. I was tipped off about it," he added, "by a big fellow with a walrus mustache."

The children exchanged glances. Had Mr. Burden done the damage himself and then tried to get the children into trouble? Since they were not sure, none of them said anything.

"What we really came here for," said Bert, "is to find a woman who has our cousin's monkey."

"Have you seen the lady?" Freddie spoke up.

The attendant's thin face broke into a smile. "Oh, yes! I saw her about half an hour ago as I was parking. Animals are my hobby, so I stopped to talk to her about it."

The children looked excited. "Do you think she's still here?" Patti asked. "Did she say where she was going next?"

The man smiled and held up his hand. "She told me she was Miss Louise North and that she was on her way to the barge canal. She's driving from here up to Canajoharie. There she'll take a private boat from Getty's Marina to Albany. It's an overnight ride."

"I hope we can catch her," said Chuck.

"Then you'd better hurry," said the attendant, "because she was in her car, ready to leave when I was talking to her."

Bert had taken a clean handkerchief from his pocket and wiped the blue chalk off the horse.

"There now," said Flossie, patting the dummy, "he's as good as new."

The children thanked the attendant for his

help and hurried to their station wagon. In a short time they had left Cooperstown and were heading north toward the canal.

"I feel sure Mr. Burden must have written on the horse," Bert spoke up. "After all, there was no one else in the museum who knew our name."

"I think so, too," said Nan. "Who else could it possibly have been?"

"I see what you mean, of course," said Mrs. Parker, frowning, "but good men like the Burdens would not do such a thing to you children."

"If they were mean they might do it to get even," said Freddie, " 'cause you wouldn't sell 'em the schoolhouse."

"Perhaps they did it to get us into trouble, so we'd be held up at the museum," Nan suggested thoughtfully. "Maybe they think we're following them."

"But why would they suppose that?" Bert asked, puzzled, "unless they *are* the spooks."

"That I can't believe," said Mrs. Parker firmly.

"I don't care about them anyway," Patti spoke up. "Let's try to catch Milly."

Mrs. Parker glanced at her watch. "We'll do our best, Patti, but Miss North has a headstart."

It was dusk when they arrived at the outskirts of Canajoharie and drove along the canal. They spotted a small white building with a sign *Getty's Marina* on the roof.

As they pulled up, the children cried out in excitement. There was a red convertible in the parking lot!

Eagerly the family piled out and hurried inside. A young man wearing a white yachting cap smiled across the counter and asked what he could do for them.

"The woman with the monkey," said Nan quickly, "where is she?"

"There she is!" cried Flossie.

The others turned to see the little girl running through the back door of the marina onto a dock. They dashed out after her and saw a blue boat speeding away. On deck was a woman in a green jacket holding a monkey in a yellow sweater.

"Milly! Milly!" Patti cried.

As the children waved and shouted, the woman waved back. But the boat sped on down the canal into the twilight.

CHAPTER XIII

CANALBOAT CLUE

"IT'S too late," said Flossie sadly. "She's gone."

"And Milly too," Patti sighed, gazing at the lights of the boat disappearing in the distance.

Putting an arm around Patti, Mrs. Parker led the children back into the marina.

"We were too late to catch Miss North," she said to the young man, "but we would like to hire a boat for an overnight trip to Albany."

The man nodded. "We have one here. Captain Jimmy Sweet will take you. If you wish, my partner can drive your car to Albany and deliver it to your hotel tomorrow afternoon. I will make reservations for you there if you wish."

"That would be a great help," said Mrs. Parker.

Bert asked, "Can you tell us Miss North's address?"

"I have it right here," said the man.

Looking at an order pad on the counter, he copied the information on a piece of paper which he gave to Bert.

Soon the travelers and their bags were aboard a trim little yacht called *The Water Baby*.

Captain Jimmy Sweet was a suntanned young man with blond hair and a beard. After giving them a hearty welcome, he introduced a husky dark-haired man who was working on deck.

"This is our first mate, Ed Malone."

"I'm the whole crew, too," said the man, grinning.

Whistling cheerfully, he hauled in the anchor, and a few moments later the white craft was cutting through the dark canal water.

"There's plenty of chow in the galley," said the captain. "Did you folks eat?"

"Not yet," said Freddie, "and I'm hungry!"

"Good," said Captain Sweet. "Mr. Malone will hustle up a meal."

A short time later passengers and captain were seated at a table on deck. The yellow lantern over the galley door cast a warm light on the white cloth.

"Turkey sandwiches and french fries coming up!" said Mr. Malone as he set down two heaping platters.

While eating hungrily, the travelers watched the dark, tree-lined shore.

"We're moving a lot faster than the old canalboats did," Bert remarked as the mate served ice cream.

Captain Sweet nodded. "We certainly are! Everything is different now. In those days the roof of the cabin was the top deck and people sat on it. But there were low bridges over the canal and whenever a boat reached one of them the steersman would shout, 'Low bridge! Everybody down!' Then all the people on the roof had to lie flat on their faces so they could go under the bridge without being swept off."

Flossie giggled. "You mean ladies in hoop skirts and everybody?"

"Everybody." Captain Sweet grinned. "The steersman carried a long horn. The biggest were about four feet, others were shorter. Every time the boat approached a lock he blew the horn to warn the lock tender he was coming."

"I'd like to do that," said Freddie. "It sounds like fun."

"What's a lock?" Flossie asked.

"It's a sort of water elevator," the captain replied. "It raises or lowers the boat from one level of the canal to another."

"And the tender is the man who looks after it," added Nan.

"When this canal was built, it was the biggest one in the whole world, wasn't it?" Bert asked.

"Yes, it was," said Captain Sweet, passing his guests a plate of cookies. "Everyone in the country was excited about it. When it was opened there were great celebrations.

"Governor De Witt Clinton and his party boarded the first boat at Buffalo," he went on, "and a cannon was fired. When the people farther down the canal heard the boom, they fired their cannon. This was repeated all along the banks. In this way word was sent to Albany that the canal was open. The message went five hundred miles in eighty-one minutes."

"That was fast for those days," said Mrs. Parker. "They had to do it that way, because it was before the telegraph, telephone, radio or television had been invented."

"Oh, it was a great day all right," said Captain Sweet. "There were bands playing along the banks, and when night came people lit huge homemade lanterns. They were called transparencies."

He explained that these were big boxes with letters cut out of the sides spelling "Erie Canal" or "De Witt Clinton." A candle or torch burned inside each one.

"They must have been bee-yoo-ti-ful," said Flossie, her eyes sparkling at the thought.

"That's not all," said Captain Sweet. "There were fireworks and dancing and parties all night long in the canal towns. I have some pictures I'll show you." He excused himself and went below deck.

A moment later a boat appeared alongside them.

"Look! That's like the one Miss North was on!" Nan exclaimed. Everyone hurried over to the rail.

"Ahoy there!" Bert called as the other craft drew abreast. A man was standing at the wheel with a boy of about fourteen.

"Ahoy yourself!" called the boy, waving and grinning.

"Do you have a monkey on board?" Freddie cried excitedly.

The man at the wheel looked over, puzzled.

"They don't understand you, Freddie," said Nan quickly.

"Do you have a monkey on board?" Bert called loudly.

At that the boy grinned and nodded. He whispered to the man, then dashed into the cabin.

"Oh, I think they have!" Patti exclaimed, clapping her hands together.

"Steady, dear," said Mrs. Parker, patting her daughter on the shoulder. "Just wait and see." But even she watched eagerly as the man from the next boat looked over from time to time, smiled, but said nothing.

A few minutes later the boy ran out. He was carrying something wrapped in canvas.

"It's Milly, I'll bet!" cried Chuck. He climbed up partway on the railing and leaned toward the other boat. "Let us have her!" he shouted.

"Here it comes!" The boy tossed the bundle toward Chuck.

Chuck lost his balance

"Catch it!" Patti cried as her brother leaned toward the flying parcel. Grabbing at it, he lost his balance.

"Yipe!" he yelled, toppling over the rail.

Quickly Bert and Nan seized their cousin and hauled him back to safety.

"Wow!" Chuck gasped, still clutching the bundle. "That was close."

"Quick, open the canvas!" cried Patti.

Eagerly Chuck unrolled the bulky wrapping. Everyone groaned. Inside was a red and yellow box of animal crackers!

As they looked up, the boy on the next boat laughed and waved. The other craft sped past them.

"They thought we were kidding," said Nan, disappointed.

Just then Captain Sweet came on deck with a big book in his hand. Quickly the children told what had happened. He peered ahead at the other yacht.

"That's not the one Miss North was on," he said. "You had the wrong boat."

For the rest of the evening the cousins sat on deck talking to Captain Sweet and looking at the book of canal pictures. Finally they went to bed in two cabins below. The boys were in one, the girls and Mrs. Parker in another.

"We're going to sleep double-deck," said Flossie happily. "I want to be up top."

"All right," said Nan. She boosted her little sister into the upper bunk. Soon everyone drifted off to sleep, listening to the soft swish of the water against the hull of the boat.

In the morning Captain Sweet woke them with a cheery whistle. Soon Mr. Malone served sizzling bacon and waffles on deck. When all of them finished breakfast the boat tied up at the dock in Albany. The twins and their cousins said good-by to the friendly skipper and mate, then took a taxi to the hotel.

They were shown to three rooms, one each for the girls, the boys, and Mrs. Parker. Afterward, they met in the lobby.

"Now we have to find Miss North," said Bert. He pulled the piece of paper from his pocket. "Oh-oh," he said, frowning. "There's one of these numbers I can't read."

The others looked at the address, but no one could decipher the scribbled figure.

"It could be one-zero-zero-six," said Flossie, "or seven-zero-zero-six."

"I guess we'll have to cover both places," said Nan. "We'll save time if we split up and take two taxis."

"Right," Mrs. Parker agreed. "The young twins and Chuck can go with me to the lower number. The rest of you take the other one." It was agreed to meet at the hotel for lunch.

They left the lobby, and fifteen minutes later the older children's cab pulled up across from a yellow brick apartment house with iron balconies.

"That's the place over there," said the driver. Bert paid the man and the cousins hopped out. They walked a short distance to the corner and waited for the traffic light to turn green. As they were crossing the street, the children saw a young woman in blue slacks step out on a first-floor balcony.

"She could be Miss North!" exclaimed Nan. "She has short blond hair."

"What'll we do?" Patti asked as they reached the curb. "If she has stolen Milly, she won't admit it."

"First we must find out if she's the right person," said Bert. "Let's go talk to her."

The three children walked along the front of the building. They paused before the balcony where the young woman was now reading a magazine. The french door into the apartment was open.

"Hello," Nan called.

The woman looked up and smiled. "Hello," she said pleasantly. "I haven't seen you in this neighborhood before. Did you just move in?"

"No, we're visitors," said Nan.

"Did you, by any chance, just come from a trip on the canal?" Bert asked.

The woman was surprised. "As a matter of fact, I did. How did you know?"

"I think we saw you along the way," said Nan.

Meanwhile Patti's heart had begun to beat

hard. This was the right woman. Looking toward the open french door, Patti had an idea.

"Milly!" she suddenly called loudly.

The woman in the chair looked startled.

"Milly, come here!" Nan called, getting the idea.

The next moment the door swung wider. A small brown furry head peered around it.

"Milly! Milly!" cried Patti. Then she stopped short and her face fell. Tears came to her eyes. "Oh, no!" she whispered. "It's the wrong monkey!"

CHAPTER XIV

THE MAGIC MAN

"MY cousin thought it was her monkey," Nan said to the young woman on the balcony. "But hers is larger than this one." Briefly she explained about the missing pet.

"What a shame!" said Miss North. "You've come all this way for nothing."

She told the children she remembered the man honking at her as she drove out of the gas station. "And a woman called and waved in the Watkins Glen parking lot. But I thought they were hailing someone else."

As Miss North spoke, Patti put her hand between the railings of the balcony and sadly took the monkey's small brown paw.

"I wish I could do something for you," the young woman said.

Bert looked thoughtful. "Maybe you can. While you were on your trip, did you see a big man with a black walrus mustache?"

Nan added, "He may have had two men with him. They were big and tall too."

Miss North shook her head slowly. "I don't remember anyone like that. Do you think he can help you find your monkey?"

"Maybe," Bert said, unwilling to repeat the children's suspicions. Then he added, "He could be in Albany by now. His office is here. His name is Burden."

Miss North looked surprised. "You mean the man who owns the Burden Amusement Company?" she asked.

"That's the one," said Nan.

"I don't know him, but I've heard about the Burden brothers," Miss North said. "They have an excellent reputation." She told the children where to find their office downtown. "The bus that goes past here stops in front of it," she added.

After thanking her, the children each shook hands with the monkey. As they said good-by, they saw the bus coming. Dashing off, they caught it at the corner.

Twenty minutes later they got out on a busy downtown street. Before them was a large office building.

"What are we going to say to Mr. Burden?" Patti asked as the three went into the lobby.

"We'll ask him if he mentioned our names to anyone in the carriage museum," Nan said. "I think we can tell by the way he answers whether he's the one who chalked those words on the horse."

"And if he did, he's probably one of the spooks," said Patti.

Nan looked worried. "But everyone says the Burdens are such good men. Suppose we're wrong?"

"I have an idea about that," said Bert. "When we see Mr. Burden I'll know if I'm right." He stopped at a candy stand at the side of the lobby to buy a package of butterscotch. "Do you know which floor the Burdens are on?" Bert asked the clerk.

"The fourth—in 420," the man replied, "but you'd better step lively." He glanced up at a wall clock. "The Burdens go out to lunch every day promptly at noon. You've only got seven minutes to catch them."

Bert thanked the man and the children hurried to a bank of elevators at one end of the hall. A crowd of people was streaming into one of the cars. As the children reached the doors they slammed shut.

"Here's another one! Come on!" Nan said. They hurried to the other end of the line, but the same thing happened.

"Here!" cried Patti. "This one!"

"No, no!" Bert exclaimed, pulling her back. "That one's an express." He pointed to the sign above it. "See? It goes straight to the tenth floor."

"If we don't get an elevator soon, it'll be too late," Patti said worriedly.

"Come on, let's walk up," Nan suggested. She rushed across the lobby and opened a door with the word *Stairs* on it. The trio found themselves in a small hallway facing a flight of concrete steps.

Bert ran up with the girls at his heels. At the landing they turned and went up another flight, then several more. The breathless girls lost count.

"Where are we?" Nan gasped.

"This is it! Fourth floor!" Bert said. He yanked open the door at the top and the children stepped into a hallway which had offices on either side. Hurrying along, they looked at the numbers on the doors.

"Four-twenty—here it is!" said Bert.

He opened the door and they walked in. Just inside, a gray-haired woman wearing a neat suit was seated at a big modern desk.

"We'd like to see Mr. Louis Burden, please," Bert said.

"I'm sorry, but you've just missed him," she said kindly. "He and his brother went out to lunch."

The children looked at one another in dismay.

"What time will they be back?" Bert asked.

"I'm not sure," the woman replied. "They may take a long time. Could I help you?"

"I'm afraid not," said Bert. "Thank you anyway."

Seeing how disappointed the children looked, the woman said, "If it's something important, why don't you try to catch them? They left only a few moments ago."

The children thanked her and hurried out the door. They dashed to the bank of elevators, but one look showed them all the cars were on floors far from this one.

"The stairs again!" exclaimed Bert.

In an instant the children were racing down, Bert in the lead. As he leaped the last two steps to the landing, a boy came around the bend carrying a large tray of coffee and sandwiches.

"Watch out!" cried Nan. The delivery boy took a quick sidestep and Bert shot past him without touching the tray.

"Where do you think you're going?" the boy asked angrily.

"Sorry!" Bert said breathlessly, pausing a moment to look back.

"You're not hurt, are you?" Nan asked anxiously.

"No, I'm okay," said the boy, frowning, "but next time, blow your horn."

The trio hurried down into the lobby. It was very crowded.

"I don't see Mr. Burden, do you?" Nan asked.

"Where do you think you're going?"
the boy asked angrily

"Maybe we missed him," said Patti.

"Come on!" said Bert. "I have an idea." He made his way back to the candy stand. "Did you see the Burden brothers come down?" he asked the clerk.

"Burden?" the man said, glancing around the lobby. "There they go!" He pointed toward the front door. "See those two fellows in plaid jackets?"

A couple of short, fat men wearing bright-colored jackets and brown hats with feather brushes were just going out the front door.

"Those are the Burden brothers?" Bert asked the clerk.

"Right." The girls stared in amazement.

"Are there more?" Bert asked.

"No. Just two," the clerk said.

"Do any other men work in that office?" Bert asked.

"Nope. Only Lou and Tom Burden. They're great little guys, always doing something for somebody."

"Thank you very much," said Bert slowly, and turned to look at the two girls. They all stepped away from the candy counter.

"It's just as I suspected," Bert said. "Mr. Walrus and his two pals are impostors!"

The girls nodded solemnly. "So we can be almost positive they're the spooks," said Nan.

After asking directions from a policeman, the children walked toward their hotel. On the way they looked in the window of a magic shop.

"We ought to come here this afternoon," Bert said, "and scout around. I've thought right along that the tricks used in the schoolhouse were professional, because they were so smooth. Maybe we could get a lead on some of them."

During lunch the older children told the others about their morning's adventure. Mrs. Parker suggested that she and Bert go and tell the Burdens about the impostors.

"All right," Bert agreed. "The others can go to the magic store."

An hour later Nan turned the handle of the shop door and stepped inside.

"Welcome to magic land," said a deep voice.

"I don't see anybody," Freddie whispered, looking around the dimly lit shop. On the counter were fake mustaches and rubber spiders. Beards and wigs were hanging on wall hooks. In a corner was a tall glass case full of costumes.

"Make yourselves at home," the voice went on, "but do not open the magic door or you will disappear." The children looked at one another and giggled.

"Where are you, voice?" Nan asked into the air.

"I'm right here." The words came from their right.

The children jumped and turned. A man had popped up from behind the counter. He was tall with a long neck and straight, black hair which hung down to his collar. There was a sly twinkle in his big, dark eyes.

"I fooled you, didn't I?" he said with a grin. "I saw you coming, so I talked to you from my microphone under the counter."

He pointed to a dark shelf above the door. "The loudspeaker's up there."

Chuck laughed. "That's a good trick!"

The man smiled and nodded. "Yes, Mr. Magic has a trick for every occasion—that's me —Mr. Magic." He tapped his chest. "What can I do for you?" he asked, coming out from behind the counter.

"We'd like to look around," said Nan.

"Go right ahead! But wait!" He put his hand on Freddie's head and said, "Young man, do you like surprises?"

Freddie grinned. "If they're fun, I do."

The man leaned over and whispered into Freddie's ear. The little boy laughed. "All right," he said, "if it won't hurt."

"It certainly will not hurt," said the man with a smile. "Come along—all of you."

He led the way behind a folding screen at one side of the shop. Before them was a door. When he opened it, Patti gasped. "My, it's dark in there!" she cried out.

"Now then," said Mr. Magic in his deepest voice, "walk right in, young man."

Freddie grinned and took a step into the

room. For a moment they could make out his form. Then the magician pressed a button beside the door and a bright light flashed. The other children jumped back, blinking and holding their hands up to their eyes. When they opened them again, they could not believe what they saw!

"Freddie's gone!" Flossie exclaimed.

"No, I'm not," said his voice.

"Where are you?" asked Nan, bewildered. After the bright light everything was darker than ever.

"I'm up here!"

The other children stared hard at the black ceiling. They could not see a thing.

CHAPTER XV

A GHOST HORN

"FREDDIE'S gone!" exclaimed Flossie.

She and the other children peered fearfully into the dark room. The tall magician chuckled, and they could hear Freddie giggling.

"Look for him again," said Mr. Magic in his deep voice.

He pressed another button and a small red light went on over the door inside the room. In the weird glow the children saw that it was all draped in black. Hanging from the ceiling was a large black bag. It was wiggling.

The magician grinned and reached behind the draperies. Pulling some ropes, he carefully lowered the black bag to the ground. The top opened and Freddie popped up.

"Ha-ha-ha! I fooled you, didn't I?" he said, as he stepped out of the crumpled sack.

"That's a great trick!" exclaimed Chuck. "How did you do it?"

"First of all, I had everything ready," said the magician. He used the pulley to raise the bag to the ceiling. "Second, the room is so dark with the black draperies that you couldn't see much. Right?"

"Right," the children chorused.

"Then two things happened at once," the tall man went on. "The light flashed, making you blink your eyes, and in that twinkling, down came the sack! It opens at the bottom, too, and—"

"—it fell right over me!" Freddie put in excitedly. "Then I held onto a handle inside and rode up. It was fun!"

"I invented that sack especially for this trick," said Mr. Magic proudly.

"I'll bet you know a lot of other ones, too," said Chuck.

The man nodded. "But this is the only secret that I tell. I love to do tricks," he went on, "and I use this one for demonstration."

"This is a 'citing place!" Flossie remarked.

The magician patted her head. "Well, look around all you want. Call me when you need help."

The children poked around the interesting shop. In a back room they found one wall covered with all kinds of false faces. On a table lay a dozen big animal-head masks.

"Aren't they marvelous!" exclaimed Nan. "You fit them on right over your own head."

Flossie was admiring the long trunk of the elephant and Freddie was examining a bull with red eyes and plastic horns. "He's fierce!" said the little boy, grinning.

"I like the dog and the cow," Patti announced.

"I'll take the giraffe!" said Chuck. "He's funny." He gazed up at the smiling head on the long, spotted neck.

On a shelf Nan saw several metal tubes with colored silk hanging from them. A sign in front said, "Handkerchief Trick."

"What thin material!" Nan exclaimed. "I guess it has to be fine so you can get lots and lots of handkerchiefs into that narrow tube."

Patti fingered a piece of black silk. "That could go through a tiny space," she said, nodding.

A thoughtful look crossed Nan's face. Her eyes grew bright with excitement. "I know what!" she said. "Suppose—"

At that moment the children heard footsteps in the shop.

"We're back again, Mr. Magic," rumbled a voice.

Flossie gasped and pulled Nan's sleeve. "It sounds like Mr. Walrus!"

"We want to buy a mask," another voice said.

"The scariest one in the whole store," added a higher voice.

Freddie and Flossie could hardly keep still for excitement. These were the two men they had overheard at the band concert!

"I have something special in the stockroom downstairs," the magician replied. "It just came in. I'll get it."

The children heard his footsteps fade away.

"This time," said Mr. Walrus, "we're going to scare those kids right out of that schoolhouse so they'll *never* come back."

"We say that every time," remarked the deep voice gloomily, "but they always come back."

"That's because of those twins," declared Mr. Walrus angrily. "Everything was going fine until they came on the scene."

"They worry me, Jack," said the high-voiced man. "They must suspect us. That's why they followed us to Cooperstown."

"Well, we fixed 'em there! While they were in trouble over the writing on the horse, we gave them the slip."

"You *hope*," said the deep voice.

"Ted," said Mr. Walrus, "you're a worry-wart. You, too, Hal."

"I can't help it," said the high voice. "Those twins are trouble."

"Yes," rumbled Mr. Walrus, "and if I catch them snooping around us again, they'll be sorry!"

The listeners heard footsteps coming back.

"Here it is!" said the magician. "A devil!"

"No good," said Mr. Walrus shortly.

"I have a whole back room full of masks," said the magician smoothly. "Why don't you step in there and take a look around?"

The children exchanged frightened looks. There was no place to hide!

"The animal heads!" Nan exclaimed softly.

Quickly she picked up the elephant and fitted it over Flossie's head. As heavy footsteps approached the door, the other children hurriedly put on the dog, giraffe, bull and cow.

"What's this?" exclaimed Mr. Walrus as he and his two companions entered the room. They looked hard at the five disguised children.

"Who are these kids?" Mr. Walrus asked suspiciously.

The magician smiled. "Just some youngsters who came into the shop."

The big man grunted. He started to lift the bull mask off Freddie. "I'll take this one," he said.

"No!" cried the little boy in a muffled voice. He held the animal mask tightly over his head. "I saw it first!"

"Wait, Jack," said Ted. "This one's better." He picked up a fierce gorilla head.

"Okay," grumbled Mr. Walrus. "That should do the trick."

The men turned and left the room. For a few

"Who are those kids?" asked Mr. Walrus suspiciously

minutes the children stood quietly with the masks on, waiting for the men to leave the shop. The voices came back clearly.

"How did your remote control box work?" the magician asked. "Did it ring the bell and shake the floor?"

"Yes, it was fine," said Mr. Walrus.

"Were your friends scared?" the magician asked pleasantly.

The man laughed hollowly. "Not scared enough," said Mr. Walrus. "That's why we need the gorilla face."

"Well, good luck," said the magician, chuckling. "Have fun!"

Hearing the men leave, the children removed the animal heads and put them back on the table.

Nan gave a sigh of relief. "That was quick thinking, Freddie," she said.

"I *knew* those fellows were the spooks!" Freddie exploded. "Wait'll we tell Bert about this!"

"I think I know something else, too," said Nan, remembering the idea she had had just before hearing Mr. Walrus speak.

"What?" Patti asked.

"How the picture of the ghost was rigged!"

"How?" the others chorused.

"With black silk—the kind used for the handkerchief trick.

"I think," Nan went on, "that two of the men

hurried ahead of us to the schoolhouse and quickly drew the spook. Then they pinned or taped the thin black cloth over it.

"On the bottom of the silk there must have been a thread or string," she continued, "which they put through that hole Freddie found in the floor. Then they ran outside and hid. When we went in we didn't notice the black curtain against the blackboard."

"I get it!" said Patti. "Just like Mr. Magic fooled us with Freddie in the black bag against the black draperies."

Nan nodded. "That's it. Meantime one of the men had run the thread out through the break in the boards under the window."

Chuck nodded excitedly. "Sure! Then the other fellow made a noise at the front door."

Nan nodded. "When we went out to see what it was, his pal pulled the thread. It yanked the silk off the blackboard, pulled it through that tiny hole in the floor, and out between the broken boards."

"Freddie was right, after all!" said Patti. "The ghost *did* go through the hole in the floor!"

"And look! Here's what the men used to draw the spook," exclaimed Flossie. She picked a bright-colored box off the shelf and held it up. It was labeled "Glow-Chalk."

Patti read the directions. "You're right, Floss.

If you put this stuff in the light for a while it will glow when you use it in the dark."

"The men could have shone a flashlight on it to make it work," Nan remarked.

"Let's buy some," suggested Freddie. "And I'd like a mustache, too," he added, picking a big black one from the shelf.

Taking the purchases with them, the children went out to the magic man. As Nan paid him, Patti asked if the three men had ever bought black silk and Glow-Chalk.

Mr. Magic looked surprised. "How did you know?"

Nan told him their story. She added that the men were suspected of taking a camera and a monkey.

The magic man's eyebrows rose high. "You mean those fellows were using all this stuff to scare you?"

"Yes," said Flossie.

The magician frowned. "I don't like that one bit. I sell my tricks for fun, not for grownups to frighten children."

"Do you know their last names or where they live?" Nan asked.

"No, I'm sorry," said the magician.

He promised that if the three men came back he would alert the police.

The children returned to their hotel. Bert and Mrs. Parker were waiting in the lobby.

Eagerly the newcomers reported what had happened.

Bert's eyes sparkled. "I wish I'd been along!"

"The Burdens were very grateful to us for telling them about the impostors," said Mrs. Parker.

"I told them all about our two mysteries and Cherry Corners," said Bert. "They were very interested."

"Now I think it's time we went home," said Mrs. Parker. "I'll call Daddy tonight and tell him when to expect us. We need to get ready for Patti's birthday party," she added, smiling.

"Two days after tomorrow," sang Flossie, clapping her hands. "I can't wait."

The travelers arrived in Cherry Corners late the next afternoon. On the hall table was a note for the children from Mr. Parker.

"Bill said for you to come down to the school-house the minute you get home. It's important."

"I wonder what's happened," Bert said. "We'd better go see."

With Cooky trotting happily at their heels, the cousins hurried through the cherry orchard. On the way Freddie put on his mustache.

They found Bill, Sally and Mary seated on the steps of the schoolhouse. "Hi!" said Bill, jumping up. "Are we glad to see you! There's been some new spooky stuff!"

The cousins looked startled. "That can't be," exclaimed Bert. "The spooks were out of town!"

"What do you mean?" Bill asked.

Before Bert could explain, Mary said, "We heard a ghost horn yesterday afternoon." Her plump face was worried.

"It was really weird," added Sally fearfully. "The noise just seemed to come out of the air!"

"Are you sure it wasn't the wind?" Nan asked.

Before Sally could answer, an eerie, quavery sound came floating down from somewhere above!

CHAPTER XVI

THE BLACK BOX

"THE ghost horn!" cried Flossie.

The startled children looked up into the air. Once again the quavery notes came floating down.

"But I don't see anything," said Patti, gazing all around.

Nan pointed to the edge of the clearing. "The sound seemed to come from above the trees over there."

"It's an awfully scary noise," said Mary, trembling.

"How do you think the spook does it?" Sally asked.

"I don't think the spook does it," Bert replied. "I started to tell you before. We know there are three fellows who have been haunting the schoolhouse. We saw them while we were on our trip."

"You did?" exclaimed Sally and Mary.

"So that's what you meant by the spooks being out of town," said Bill. His eyes were sparkling with excitement. "Who are they? Tell us about them!"

The travelers reported their adventures. When they finished, Bill gave a low whistle.

"Now we have to look for an electronic box," he remarked.

"Maybe the horn was done by remote control, too," said Sally.

"I don't think so. If it were, the magic man would have mentioned it," Nan replied.

"Where do you think the box is hidden?" Chuck asked.

"Not in the schoolhouse, that's for sure," said Bert. "We've gone over it inch by inch."

"I'll bet I know!" said Flossie. "Remember my spook in the bush—the one you said was a rabbit?"

The others turned to look at her. "I think it was one of the bad men fixing the 'tronic box."

"Maybe she's right," said Nan.

"Let's go look!" said Chuck excitedly.

"Wait!" said Bert. "If we find the box we'll test it. Some of you stay here and see what happens. Nan, you and Bill come with me."

Bert led the way to the huge clump of brush on the canal bank.

"Let's each take a side, creep in and search for the box," he directed. "We'll meet underneath in the middle."

"I've found something," Nan said

The trio crawled under the branches. After a few minutes Nan called, "Come here, quick!"

Bert and Bill pushed through the twigs and leaves until they came to Nan. She was kneeling beside a hole in the ground.

"I've found something!" she said.

Down in the pit was a black metal box with buttons on it.

"This is it, all right!" exclaimed Bert.

At that moment they heard excited voices, and Freddie cried, "You give that back, Danny Rugg!"

The listeners in the brush exchanged disgusted looks. "It's your old friend again," said Bill. "Everybody in town knows him by now."

A grin came over Bert's face. "Let's give him a scare," he said softly. "You wait here and when I whistle, press the buttons."

Bill grinned. "I get it!" he said as Nan giggled.

Bert crept from under the brush and hurried to the front of the schoolhouse. Danny was strutting up and down wearing Freddie's fake mustache. The others watched indignantly.

"You ought to be ashamed of yourself, Danny," Patti scolded.

"Danny likes that kid stuff," said Bert.

The bully scowled. "What do you mean?"

"Well, anybody can grab a mustache away from a little boy," said Bert. "When are you going to show some real nerve?"

"I don't know what you're talking about,"

said Danny, patting the mustache tighter under his nose.

Bert shrugged and turned away. "I guess he's scared," he said to the others.

Danny frowned. "Scared of what?"

"To go into the haunted schoolhouse, of course," said Bert coolly.

Danny grinned. "Haunted! You believe that stuff?"

"If you're not afraid, why don't you go in?" Bert asked, winking at the others.

"Yes, why don't you go in?" asked Freddie.

"Go ahead," said Patti, "unless you're too scared."

"We dare you," said Sally.

"Chicken!" Freddie added and Chuck cackled like a hen.

As the girls giggled, Danny's face grew red.

Bert smiled. "Danny would rather play baby games."

"Oh yeah?" the big boy said angrily. He yanked the mustache off and threw it at Freddie. "There, take your old lip rug. I'll show you who's scared." With that, he marched up the school steps and tried to open the door.

"Wait a minute!" said Patti sweetly, taking the keys from her pocket. "I have to unlock the door first."

While Danny glowered she opened both locks. "Okay, in you go." She backed down and stood with the others.

Danny stuck out his chest and walked through the doorway. They heard him stomp into the classroom.

"Okay," he yelled. "Here I am! Now where's your old spook?"

At that Bert gave a sharp whistle. The school bell began to clang and the building shook. With a wild yell Danny shot out the door and dashed up through the orchard.

As he disappeared, the children collapsed in laughter. Minutes later Bill came running up with Nan. She was carrying the black box.

"That took care of Danny all right!" said Patti, when they had all stopped laughing. "Now what'll we do about the spooks?"

Nan grinned. "Let's leave them a message."

She beckoned the others to follow her into the schoolhouse. There she reached into her pocket and took out the box of Glow-Chalk. As soon as the others saw it, they grinned.

"What'll we say?" Nan asked.

For a moment they all thought of various messages. Then Patti said, "To our electronic spooks: You can't scare us out!"

"Signed, The Pet Club," Flossie added.

The others laughed and Bert printed the message on the board.

"Now they'll have to give up and go away," said Freddie, " 'cause they'll know we're on to them."

"Yes, we've solved part of the mystery," said

Nan. "But the black box only does two tricks. We still can't explain the horn."

"Or find the treasure," Bill put in.

With a sudden gasp Bert snapped his fingers. "I've got it! I'll bet the horn is the treasure!"

"What!" exclaimed Chuck. There was a chorus of excited questions.

"I say it's an old canal horn!" Bert declared.

"Why do you think that?" asked Nan.

"Remember the round clean place in the dust in the tower? A horn standing on its bell-end would leave a spot like that."

"Of course!" exclaimed his twin. "We know that whatever Milly carried away that night was metal! Oh, I feel sure you're right!"

"Then if the horn's around here, maybe Milly is too," said Patti eagerly.

"But we can't be sure of that, Patti," Bert told her kindly. "Someone might have taken it away from her."

"Who do you think has been blowing it?" asked Mary.

"And where can the person be when he does it?" added Sally.

"Who knows?" said Bert. "We'll have to keep working on the problem." As he spoke, a whistle sounded up on the hill.

"Supper," said Chuck. "Let's go!"

Patti grinned. "I'll leave the door unlocked, so it'll be easier for the spooks to get in."

Calling good-by, the children went their separate ways. When the cousins arrived home, they showed Mr. and Mrs. Parker the electronic box. The couple listened in amazement as Bert explained how the tricks had been worked.

"And we left a surprise for the bad men," said Flossie. Eagerly she told about the message on the blackboard.

"We also think we know what the treasure is," said Nan. She reported how they had decided.

"That was very good thinking, Bert," said Mr. Parker. "In fact, I congratulate all of you children! I'll report this to the police and turn the box over to them."

"You've made great progress with your detective work," Mrs. Parker added.

"But we haven't got Milly back," Patti wailed.

Her mother put an arm around her. "Let's forget about mysteries for a while, Patti. The stores are open tonight and we must do our shopping for your party."

After supper the children and Mrs. Parker walked to Main Street. While Patti and her mother bought food, the others went to a book and gift shop to buy birthday presents.

Nan picked a charm bracelet with a little green monkey on it. Flossie chose a record, and Bert and Freddie together bought a big book of animal photographs. Chuck bought two turtles and a special plastic bowl for them.

"Maybe these will take Patti's mind off Milly," he said.

As the twins and Chuck started home, Bert

remembered that he needed batteries for his flashlight. He went back to the drugstore and bought them.

"Never can tell when I might need this again," he thought as he slid them into the pencil light.

Next day the children were busy wrapping packages and getting the games ready. Mrs. Parker baked a big cake, which Nan and Flossie decorated with pink-and-white icing.

After supper Nan said, "I think we should take a look around the schoolhouse. Maybe we could pick up a lead on the ghost horn."

Mrs. Parker looked doubtful. "Oh, please, Mother," Patti begged. "If those men have seen the sign we left, they won't bother us any more."

"All right," said Mrs. Parker, "but be back before dark."

A short while later the six children were trooping down through the orchard. It was gloomy because the trees shut out the evening light.

"It's kind of spooky here," said Flossie uneasily, taking Nan's hand. Suddenly the eerie sound of the horn floated up from below.

"It's near the school again!" Bert exclaimed.

The children began to run. As they neared the bottom of the hill, they glimpsed a bright flash through the trees ahead.

"What's going on?" Chuck cried.

"Come on!" said Bert. "Hurry!"

But as he sprinted ahead, Bert stumbled over a rock and fell sprawling. Chuck, at his heels, went down on top of him. "Oof!" yelped Bert.

The girls and Freddie stopped, panting. "Are you hurt?" Nan asked. She and Patti tried to help the boys to their feet.

"I'm okay," said Chuck, jumping up.

Bert sat up, holding his side. "I'll be—all right," he said, gasping. "It just knocked the breath out of me." As he stood up, the children heard the roar of a motor.

Bert took a deep breath. "Let's go!" he said. He dashed off again with the others at his heels.

Moments later the children burst into the clearing and stopped short. *They could not believe their eyes!*

"The schoolhouse!" cried Flossie. "It's gone!"

CHAPTER XVII

A DISCOVERY

"THERE it goes!" Bert exclaimed, pointing to a huge flatbed truck which was roaring down the towpath. The little school building was on it.

"The spooks have stolen our clubhouse!" cried Chuck.

At the same moment Patti spied a small dark figure in a yellow sweater clinging to the belfry. "Milly!" she cried. "Milly, come back!"

Bert and Nan were already racing after the truck, trying to get the license number. As the other children caught up with them, the two red taillights disappeared around a bend.

"No use!" said Bert, panting to a stop. "Their license plates were covered."

"They have Milly!" exclaimed Patti. "We *have* to catch that truck!"

"We'll call the police," said Nan.

The children pounded back down the path and up through the orchard. They burst into the house shouting the news.

Mr. and Mrs. Parker listened to the story in amazement.

Mr. Parker went to telephone the police. "They'll let us know when they find the thieves," he said after he hung up.

"It should be easy," said Freddie, " 'cause nobody could miss that big schoolhouse." But by bedtime there had been no word of the truck.

"Maybe the men have hidden it," said Bert.

"I wish we could look for it too," said Nan.

"We will," decided Mrs. Parker. "Tomorrow morning."

Patti said nothing, but the others knew she was worried about her pet.

Next day the children were awake early. They hurried to the breakfast table where everyone sang "Happy Birthday" to Patti. Then her mother and father each gave her a hug and kiss.

"Good luck with your search!" said Mr. Parker.

An hour later the children piled into the station wagon with Mrs. Parker. Even Cooky went along.

All morning the searchers rode through the countryside around Cherry Corners asking townspeople and farmers whether they had seen the monkey or the truck with the schoolhouse.

"The thieves probably hid it under a big tarpaulin or something," Bert suggested.

No one had seen a sign of the stolen building, the truck, or the monkey.

Shortly before noon Mrs. Parker drove home

again. After a light lunch everyone dressed for Patti's birthday party, but it was hard to work up any enthusiasm for it.

All the children in the Pet Club came. They played many exciting games and there were prizes for everyone. Afterward Mrs. Parker served ice cream and the big, beautiful birthday cake with twelve candles on it.

"Make a wish!" exclaimed some of the children as Patti took a deep breath.

POOF! She blew hard and all the candles went out. Everybody knew that Patti was wishing she could find Milly.

That evening Bert asked permission for the cousins to follow the tire tracks of the truck along the towpath.

"The police did that," said Mr. Parker.

"Maybe we could pick up a clue they missed," Nan suggested. "Please let us try."

"Well, all right," said Mr. Parker. "But stay together."

"And be sure that you are home before dark," his wife added.

The children raced to the canal. Wide tire tracks with a zigzag pattern on them showed in patches of soft earth. The trail led down the path, then swerved through a meadow of high grass and disappeared on the highway.

"We don't even know which direction the truck went," Chuck said gloomily.

"Are there any side roads near here where it might be hidden?" Bert asked.

"There's one about half a mile to our right," said Patti.

"Let's take a look at it."

Single file, the children followed him along the shoulder of the highway. They were careful to keep away from the fast-moving traffic.

"This is it, I guess," said Bert, turning down a narrow lane that led into a woods. The six walked slowly, their eyes on the stony ground.

"Here!" cried Freddie. He pointed to a zig-zag pattern in a section of mud.

Excited, the children hurried on and soon saw a wide field to their right. In the middle of it stood a big gray frame building with a huge red cherry painted on the side.

"What's that?" Flossie asked.

"That's where the old Lolly Company used to be," Patti replied. "It has been empty for simply ages."

"Years ago the fruit growers around here sold their cherries to that company," Chuck said. "They were packed in this building and shipped out on the highway or on the canal."

"That place's big enough to hide a truck in," said Bert. "Let's go over and investigate."

The children struck off through the high grass. As they approached the weather-worn building, they saw that the big painted cherry was faded and peeling. Rounding the corner to the back they stopped short in surprise.

There stood a huge truck. A tarpaulin covered something very large!

"We've found our clubhouse!" exclaimed Freddie.

"Shh!" whispered Bert sharply. "The men might be around."

He and Nan slipped through the tall weeds to the front of the truck and looked into the cab. No one was there. They ran back to the others.

"Okay!" said Bert. "We'd better call the police right away. There's no telling when the men might come back and drive it away."

Just then there sounded the ting-a-ling of a little bell.

"Listen!" Flossie whispered. "That's coming from under the cover!"

"We'd better take a look inside the schoolhouse," Bert said softly.

"I didn't bring my key," said Patti.

"We left the door open," said Nan. "Maybe it's still that way."

Bert climbed onto the truck and lifted the heavy tarpaulin. The others followed.

"It's so dark," Flossie whispered. Bert took out his flashlight and turned it on. The padlock still hung loose. Bert tried the door and found it unlocked.

Stepping into the cloakroom, he flashed his beam around. It was empty. Quietly he led the way into the schoolroom. As his light hit the teacher's desk, Patti gave a joyful cry.

"Milly!"

The monkey was seated on the desk with a

Bert led the way into the dark schoolhouse

bell in her paw. Bert's camera hung around her neck.

Patti ran to the platform and the little animal leaped into her arms. As Milly chattered and rang her bell, the children petted her.

"Do you think the men caught her again and put her in here?" Nan asked.

"Maybe," said Bert, "but she might have come in by herself through the belfry."

"This is the bell that Bert had on the bananas," said Flossie, taking it from the monkey.

"Okay, Milly," said Bert, "give me back my camera." He took it from her and hung it around his own neck. "Now let's go and—"

He stopped speaking, and the others gasped. They had heard voices outside!

"It's the bad men!" Freddie whispered.

"Where is this place we're going?" asked the man with the high voice.

"I told you, Hal," replied the deep-voiced one. "It's a hidden glen up north—miles from here. Jack wants us to drive the truck there and leave it. He'll pick us up in the car."

"That's crazy, Ted," said Hal. "I don't see why we can't take the truck straight to the Restoration."

"You're some dummy, then," rumbled Ted. "The police are looking for this schoolhouse. We have to keep it hidden until they stop searching."

"I'll be glad when this whole job is over,"

complained Hal. "Those Bobbsey twins make me nervous."

"They weren't our only bad luck," came the deep voice. "Stealing that monkey was a mistake."

"Don't I know it! That creature's caused me plenty of trouble!"

"That was your own fault," said Ted. "Your orders were to take the camera off its neck and let the animal go in the woods where the kids wouldn't find it. Instead you forgot to remove the camera and you stuck the box up a chimney. Pretty stupid!"

"I couldn't help it," whined the other man. "I heard the children coming and I panicked. I went back that night, but the monkey was gone." He sighed. "Not only that, it wouldn't surprise me if she took my keycase. She could have hidden it under her sweater."

"At least you got it back. I never did find my new screwdriver. I lost it while I was working on that electronic box."

"But you didn't have to hide under the bush and push the buttons. Or yell 'help' to decoy the kids," said Hal unhappily.

"No, but I had to crouch in the weeds and pull the string to drag that silk off the blackboard," replied Ted, "and I had to have the skeleton key made for the schoolhouse."

"All of that just to get this old building! I say it wasn't worth the trouble."

"So do I," Ted agreed. "But you know brother Jack. Once he gets an idea he won't give up."

"And he'll be mad if we're late," said Hal uneasily. "We'd better go."

"Wait a minute!" said his companion. "I think we'd better check inside that schoolhouse to be sure there's nothing there that can slide around."

The frightened children looked at one another. The next moment they felt a jolt as the men climbed onto the truck.

Bert glanced around frantically. "Quick! Behind the teacher's desk!" he whispered.

The children scuttled underneath as Bert turned off his flashlight. Patti hugged the monkey tightly and hoped she would be quiet.

The next moment the door opened and heavy footsteps clumped into the schoolroom. The beam of a flashlight swept around. The children held their breath.

"Okay!" said Ted. "This stuff won't shift."

"Wait!" said Hal softly. "How come the door was unlocked? Maybe there's somebody in here."

"No," the other replied. "Jack left it that way. He was so mad when he found the message on the board from those kids that he rushed out without stopping for anything. He was wild!"

The footsteps went away. Then the door

slammed, and the padlock was snapped shut. The shaken children crawled out of hiding.

"What'll we do?" whispered Freddie.

Before anyone could answer, the motor roared and the truck lurched off.

CHAPTER XVIII

LANTERN SIGNAL

"HOW are we going to get out of here?" Flossie asked in a shaky voice.

"We aren't," said Bert grimly, "until the truck stops."

As the schoolhouse bounced hard, the children sat down hurriedly. Soon the riding was easier.

"We must be on the highway now," Chuck whispered.

"I wonder how far they're taking us," Patti said uneasily as she held Milly on her lap. "Mommy and Daddy'll be so worried!"

It seemed hours before they felt the truck swing off onto a bumpy road. After making several turns, it suddenly stopped.

"Here we are!" came Ted's voice from the cab.

Next the children heard Mr. Walrus's voice. "Come on, fellows," he called. "Let's go! I'm parked out on the road."

"Where are we heading now?" asked Hal.

"The Happy Holiday Motel," said Mr. Walrus. His voice grew fainter as the men walked away.

"How are we ever going to get out of here?" Nan asked. "The door is padlocked and all the windows are stuck tight."

"Maybe I could climb out through the belfry," said Bert, "and go for help."

"That's a good idea!" said Chuck.

Bert carried the teacher's chair into the cloakroom. As the others watched, he stepped onto it, leaped forward and caught hold of the edge of the open trapdoor. With a grunt he pulled himself up into the belfry. He clambered past the bell and squeezed out a side opening onto the roof.

The tarpaulin lay heavily on top of him. Grasping the wooden turret with one hand, he pulled the covering up with the other. As he wriggled out from under it, he saw the sky was bright with stars.

"Where are we?" called Nan from below.

"In a deep, narrow canyon."

Patti spoke up. "You'll probably have to walk a long distance to get help."

"Wait a minute!" exclaimed Nan. "Bert!" she called. "Can you climb to the top of the canyon?"

The boy ran his flashlight beam over the jagged rock wall. "I think so. Why?"

"You could signal from up there. Remember

"I hope they can see it," Bert thought

those lanterns the people showed when the Erie Canal was opened?"

"Transparencies," said Bert.

"Yes," said Nan. "We'll make one by cutting out the letters SOS in the side of Milly's hatbox. If you hold it up someone might see it."

"Great," called Bert. "Hurry and do it."

"That's a cool idea!" exclaimed Freddie.

"You can use my scout knife," said Chuck, digging it out of his pocket.

Freddie felt his way through the dark schoolroom to the hatbox and brought it back.

Working as quickly as she could, Nan cut a large SOS in the side of the circular box. Then she stood on the chair and handed it up to Bert, who was leaning down to take it.

"Wish me luck," he said and squeezed out of the belfry again, carrying the box by the string. He walked to the roof edge, close to the canyon wall. With one big step he was on a rock ledge. Luckily the shelves were close together. It was almost like going up giant stone steps.

"Made it!" Bert muttered breathlessly as he scrambled over the top.

He was delighted to see the lights of cars moving along a highway about a mile away. Quickly he took the lid off the hatbox. Keeping the box up high in one hand, he held the flashlight inside with the other. Then he slowly walked back and forth across the cliff top.

"I hope they can see it this far," he thought.

After a while he heard a siren below. Bert looked into the canyon and saw a car with a red light on top! The police!

"Hey, up there! What's going on?" called a voice.

"There are children locked in the schoolhouse on the truck!" Bert shouted.

While he cautiously climbed down the cliff with the hatbox, the policemen broke open the padlock and let the prisoners out. By the time Bert had reached the ground, the officers had been told the whole story.

One of them was a stern-faced man with gray hair. He said his name was Craig. The other, Digby, was young and square-jawed.

"This is the wildest tale I've ever heard," Digby remarked.

"You're sure it's all true?" Officer Craig asked the children.

"Yes, sir," they chorused.

"I think we'd better go to the Happy Holiday Motel," said Officer Craig. "You can identify the men for us."

The children piled into the police car with Patti carrying the monkey. As they drove out of the canyon, Officer Craig said that they had seen Bert's SOS sign while they were riding along the highway.

"I must say that was a great idea," said Digby. "You kids have a lot of imagination."

Fifteen minutes later they pulled up in front

of a long red motel. The three men were summoned to the lobby. They did not blink an eye when they saw the children.

"May we see your identification?" said Officer Craig.

The men exchanged surprised looks.

"I don't know what this is all about, officer," said Mr. Walrus politely, "but we're glad to help." Smiling, the three produced drivers' licenses which showed that they were Jack, Lou and Carl Burden.

"Those are fake licenses," Bert spoke up. "We met the real Burden brothers in Albany. There are only two of them."

"I don't know what these children are talking about!" Mr. Walrus exclaimed. "We've never seen them before in our lives."

The cousins' hearts sank as they saw the policemen frowning at them. The men were excellent actors! How could the children prove their story was true?

Suddenly Bert remembered the flash in the air just before they discovered that the schoolhouse had been stolen. He had a wild idea! Quickly he looked at the flash attachment on his camera. Sure enough, the bulb had been used!

"Wait!" he exclaimed. Carefully he pulled the finished photograph from the back of his camera. A grin spread over his face.

"There's the proof!" He showed the picture to the policemen. Both officers' eyebrows shot up. It was a snapshot of the thieves jacking the schoolhouse onto the truck!

"You men are under arrest," said Officer Craig.

As the trio stared, dumbfounded, the policemen swiftly placed handcuffs on them.

"The monkey took your picture," said Bert, showing it to them. The three men groaned.

"Can you imagine!" Nan exclaimed. "Milly must have been in a tree playing with the camera and snapped the shutter by accident!"

Angrily Mr. Walrus confessed that his real name was Sharpe.

"Before I offered to buy the schoolhouse, I knew the kids were using it for their club," he said, "and I figured we might have to scare 'em out of it. I gave the Burdens' name, knowing nobody would suspect them of spook tricks."

"It was easy," said Hal unhappily, "because we already had the fake drivers' licenses. We got 'em when we lost our own for speeding."

Bert turned to Jack Sharpe. "You were the man I discovered on the roof, weren't you?"

The thief scowled. "I wanted to search the house for that treasure," he said, "but you stopped me."

"And your next stop is jail," put in Officer Craig.

It was after midnight when the children and crestfallen prisoners arrived at Cherry Corners in squad cars. Mr. and Mrs. Parker had been called and were waiting at police headquarters. There were also reporters and a television unit from a nearby city.

"We were so worried!" exclaimed Mrs. Parker. She hugged each of them. Standing before the cameras, the children told of their adventures. The local police were amazed. The Parkers looked proud.

"This story's going on my front page!" said Mr. Parker, as his news photographer shot the scene.

"Milly's afraid of flashbulbs," said Patti as the monkey squirmed in her arms.

"I'll bet she scared herself right out of that tree when she took the thieves' picture," said Bert. "She probably leaped onto the roof of the schoolhouse!"

"I guess she was in the big oak," said Patti. "That's the closest to it."

Later, on the way home, Nan suddenly said, "You know what? I think the canal horn is up in a tree!" She reminded them that they had heard it just before the camera flashed. "I'll bet Milly was blowing it."

The others were excited by the idea, and could hardly wait to search.

In the morning the whole family hurried down to the clearing. Freddie was boosted up into the big oak. There he found the old horn stuck among the high branches.

They all examined it eagerly. The horn was

about a foot and a half long and made of battered tin. It was not very heavy. On the side was painted a small oval picture of the *Erie Belle*.

"It's such a pretty boat!" said Flossie. "I wish we could ride on one like it."

With Nan carefully carrying the treasure, they returned to the house. On the way, Patti spoke up.

"Daddy, I've been thinking that the schoolhouse ought to belong to the town and be open to the public."

"That's right," said Chuck. "The Pet Club could meet in our playroom."

Their parents both praised the idea, and later the club members agreed.

That evening after dinner, the doorbell rang. Nan answered and was astonished to see two short stout men in red plaid jackets and caps. The Burden brothers!

"Please come in!" said Nan and called everyone to the living room to meet the visitors.

Mr. Parker shook hands with them, then said: "Children, I have a surprise for you. Mr. Lou Burden called me this afternoon. After we talked, I called the Town Council. Mr. Burden and his brother are going to be partners in the Cherry Festival. They will pay for a new *Erie Belle* to give rides to tourists. The O'Neals and a work crew are starting to build it."

As the children exclaimed in delight, Mr. Lou Burden spoke up. "We came down here to thank the young detectives personally for catching the rascals who were using our name. Each of you six children will receive a small model of the *Erie Belle* as a keepsake."

"Also, we'd like you to be in the opening pageant," said Tom Burden. "After seeing you on television, lots of people will come to Cherry Corners," he added. "Wait and see!"

Two weeks later, on the opening day of the Festival, the shiny new canalboat was moored near the schoolhouse. Crowds lined the banks. In the front were all the cousins' friends. Mr. and Mrs. Bobbsey, who had arrived the day before to take the twins home, were beaming proudly as their children boarded the packet.

The girls stood on the roof deck, their brightly colored hoop skirts billowing in the wind and the ribbons on their bonnets fluttering. Milly, dressed in the same way, held Flossie's hand.

Bert, in a captain's uniform, was in the bow. Freddie was steersman in the stern. He wore a flat hat, long trousers, and carried the old canal horn.

Meanwhile Chuck in dungarees had run to his place on the towpath beside a team of four white horses. Cooky followed at his heels.

At Bert's signal, Chuck picked up the long reins and flicked them. As the horses started to pull the boat, Freddie blew the horn loudly. The people applauded and shouted.

"They're cheering for you Bobbseys," said Patti, smiling, " 'cause you put Cherry Corners on the map!"

"We all did it together," said Nan, "so everybody wave."

"You, too, Milly," said Flossie.

As the girls fluttered their handkerchiefs, the little monkey, chattering, did the same.

DETACH ALONG DOTTED LINE AND MAIL IN ENVELOPE WITH PAYMENT